Hi! I'm Tash. I love, love, love my new school, Riverside Academy for Girls. I love everything about it: the lessons, every single one of them; playing in the Year Seven netball and hockey teams (I'm netball captain!); my new best friends, Dani, Lissa and Ali. Especially Ali.

But most of all I love the fact that it's nice and safe and predictable.

Not like home. I never know what to expect there any more. I wish I could talk to my friends about it but I can't. I promised I wouldn't.

It's not fair. I don't like keeping things from them. We said we'd tell each other everything.

But I'm not allowed.

Books by Chris Higgins

The Secrets Club series (in reading order)

ALICE IN THE SPOTLIGHT

THE TRUTH ABOUT TASH

Chris Higgins

The Secrets Club

The Truth about Tash

PUFFIN

For Vinny, Zac, Ella and Jake.
Thanks for the advice, Lucy, my netball star.

PUFFIN BOOKS

Published by the Penguin Group
Penguin Books Ltd, 80 Strand, London WC2R ORL, England
Penguin Group (USA) Inc., 375 Hudson Street, New York, New York 10014, USA
Penguin Group (Canada), 90 Eglinton Avenue East, Suite 700, Toronto, Ontario, Canada M4P 2Y3
(a division of Pearson Penguin Canada Inc.)
Penguin Ireland, 25 St Stephen's Green, Dublin 2, Ireland (a division of Penguin Books Ltd)
Penguin Group (Australia), 707 Collins Street, Melbourne, Victoria 3008, Australia
(a division of Pearson Australia Group Pty Ltd)
Penguin Books India Pvt Ltd, 11 Community Centre, Panchsheel Park, New Delhi – 110 017, India
Penguin Group (NZ), 67 Apollo Drive, Rosedale, Auckland 0632, New Zealand
(a division of Pearson New Zealand Ltd)
Penguin Books (South Africa) (Pty) Ltd, Block D, Rosebank Office Park, 181 Jan Smuts Avenue, Parktown
North, Gauteng 2193, South Africa

Penguin Books Ltd, Registered Offices: 80 Strand, London WC2R ORL, England

puffinbooks.com

First published 2013
001

Text copyright © Chris Higgins, 2013
Illustration of Tash copyright © Helen Huang, 2013
Chapter illustrations copyright © Puffin Books, 2013
All rights reserved

The moral right of the author and illustrator has been asserted

Set in 13.5/17.5pt Baskerville by Palimpsest Book Production Limited,
Falkirk, Stirlingshire
Printed in Great Britain by Clays Ltd, St Ives plc

British Library Cataloguing in Publication Data
A CIP catalogue record for this book is available from the British Library

ISBN: 978-0-141-33523-0

www.greenpenguin.co.uk

ALWAYS LEARNING   **PEARSON**

Chapter 1

I'm chatting away nineteen to the dozen, sipping my cappuccino and loving the whole cafe scene, when Ali, my very best friend ever, suddenly starts giggling.

'What?'

Lissa and Dani stare at me then burst out laughing.

'What is it?' I say, bewildered. 'What is wrong with all of you?'

For some reason the others seem to find this hilarious.

'What is wrong with *us*?' squeals Lissa.

At last, Ali takes pity on me and splutters, 'You've got a moustache!'

'Tash – has – got – a – ta-ash!' sings Dani and they all fall about again. The whole cafe is looking at us.

'Is that all?' I jump up to look in the wall mirror behind us and study the line of cappuccino froth adorning my upper lip. To be fair it is quite impressive. I turn from side to side, admiring it. 'I think it suits me; I look like Grumpy Griffiths,' I say, which sets them all off again. But then I wipe it off and sit back down because people are staring.

Grumpy Griffiths is our ancient maths teacher at Riverside Academy for Girls where we all met for the first time in September. Not that long ago really. Weird to think that less than two months ago none of us knew each other and now we're best mates. The Gang of Four, Mrs Waters, our PE teacher, calls us.

It's the start of half term and we've got together in town for a coffee to celebrate. It's also the morning after our school 'Fashion with a Conscience' show and the first time ever that I've managed to meet up with the girls outside school, even though Ali is forever asking me to. I usually make excuses because it's a bit difficult at home. I can't leave Mum alone with the boys for too long.

But this morning Mum threaded new beads into my hair, bright shiny ones to match my top, and practically pushed me out of the door. 'Go on, Tasheika!' she said. 'I'll be fine. Go and chat about the show with your friends.'

I'd told her all about it when I got home last night. She'd sat up waiting for me, even though she'd been too exhausted after work to come and watch me. I'm not surprised she's tired out: she's got three jobs! I wish she could've seen me though, parading down the catwalk in her evening dress and everyone clapping. We were supposed to keep our faces straight but I couldn't; I was grinning from ear to ear! I felt like a real model. It was amazing.

The show took place in the Great Hall at school and there was music and flashing lights and a catwalk and stalls selling recycled clothes and jewellery. Everyone came; it was standing room only. Except Mum, but it wasn't her fault.

It was brilliant. And guess who organized it? Ali! You'd never think she had it in her to pull off something like that.

She didn't do it all on her own. Lissa gave her a hand and Austen, her friend from primary school, did too. But most of all, her sister helped her. Only we didn't find out who her sister was until she turned up at the fashion show last night.

It only turns out that Nikki Grimes, big sister of Alice Grimes (my bezzie!), is actually Alana de Silva – the most amazing model with attitude ever to appear on the catwalk (and in all the gossip magazines!). Ali never told us about her famous sister because she was embarrassed by some of the stuff she gets up to.

'I'm really sorry I kept her a secret from you all,' she said, and she'd looked so ashamed we forgave her immediately.

Ali is the complete opposite to Alana. (I'm *never* going to call her Nikki!) She's shy and quiet, like my brother Marlon. Not like me. I think that's why Ali and I are friends: we're two different parts of a jigsaw puzzle that fit together perfectly.

I glance at my watch and sigh. It's been fab. We've spent all morning gabbling on, the four of us trying to outdo each other as we recalled the best moments of last night, and I've talked and laughed myself silly. But now it's time to go.

'I'd better get home,' I say.

Ali's face falls. 'Do you have to?'

'Yeah, I told my mum I'd be back for lunch.'

'I'll come with you,' she says and jumps to her feet. Then she opens her arms wide and scoops the three of us into them for a big group hug.

4

'No more secrets,' she says. 'Promise?'

We squeeze each other tight and make a solemn vow to each other.

'NO MORE SECRETS.'

Chapter 2

Ali and I walk home together from town, chatting all the way. We live sort of near each other, only she lives in a semi-detached house with a garden on one side of the bypass and I live on the other side on the estate, in one of the tower blocks. You can see for miles from our flat; it's like being on an ocean-liner. Not that I've ever been on one, but Mum has, when she was a little girl and she came over from Jamaica to live with her aunty. Poor Mum. It didn't work out and she ended up in care all alone.

She's not all alone any more though. She's got us now. Me and Marlon and Devon and Keneil. Not Dad. He left a while ago, just after Keneil was born. Come to think of it, he wasn't around that much before. Devon can't really remember him. I can though, and Marlon can too. Dad was

6

tall and handsome and he used to chuck Marlon and Devon up in the air and call me his princess and he laughed a lot, very deep and very loud.

'That was fun,' I say, meaning the cafe, because thinking about Dad makes me feel sad.

'Let's do it again,' says Ali. 'Just the two of us!'

'You bet!' I glow inside. She does like me best after all.

My big fear is that Ali will end up best friends with Lissa instead of me. She's spent loads of time with her lately, planning the fashion show. They're on the School Council together, that's why; the fashion show was a fundraising event. But here's the good thing: Ali never told Lissa about her sister either, even though she had lots of opportunity to do so. Thank goodness. I'd have been gutted if she'd confided in her instead of me.

'Tomorrow?' she says immediately. 'Or you can come round my house if you want. Nikki will be there in the afternoon.'

'Really? OMG!' I can't believe my luck. I am actually going to meet the fantastic Alana de Silva properly, in person. When she made a special guest appearance at our fashion show last night I couldn't believe my eyes. I'm a huge fan of hers. Then I hesitate and Ali's face falls.

'It's all right,' she says glumly. 'I 'spect you're busy.'

Poor Ali. She thinks I'm about to make an excuse. Whenever she asks me to do things with her out of school I say no. She thinks I don't want to see her, but I do!

The trouble is I'm needed at home. But I'm not allowed to tell her that. Mum says it's our business and no one else's.

I wouldn't blame Ali a bit if she went off with Lissa after all.

'I dunno. I might be able to make it.' I do a quick calculation. Mum doesn't work on Sundays. We go to church in the morning, then, in the afternoon after dinner, I've been giving her a hand with the housework because she's not been right. It's been going on since summer. She's worn out all the time and she's got clumsy too. She's forever tripping up or dropping things.

'I'm getting old!' she says, but she's not, she's only thirty-two. Compared to my friends' mums she's really young. Lissa's mother is so old she says she can't remember how old she actually is. She comes to all our netball and hockey matches to watch Lissa play and she sounds like the queen or that woman who used to be prime minister in the olden days. She was at the fashion show last night (Lissa's mother, I mean, not the queen or the woman prime minister), sat behind Ali's mum and dad. Dani's mum was there too; she'd come straight from work, only I didn't get to meet her.

I wish *my* mum could've been there.

But she seemed better today. And she's forever telling me to go out and meet up with my nice new friends. She's so proud of the fact that I got a scholarship to go to Riverside Academy. And I have got all next week to give her a hand. And I *soooo* want to meet Alana de Silva properly.

'No, it's all right, I can come,' I say quickly, before I change my mind, and Ali's face lights up.

'Brilliant! D'you know where my house is?'

'I think so.'

'Tell you what, I'll meet you on the bridge at three. Yay! I can't wait!'

I wave goodbye to Ali and as soon as she's out of sight I break into a run. I need to get home to give Mum a hand. I don't mind. I'm used to dashing everywhere.

On weekdays we have a system. In the morning, Mum gets up first and sets the breakfast out for us and sees to Keneil. Then she gets the rest of us up, passes him over to me and leaves for work. I make sure Marlon and Devon are ready for school, then we leave the house together and they go off in one direction and I go the other way to drop Keneil off at nursery. Sometimes, if things go wrong, I'm late for school, but I haven't got into trouble yet, though Miss Webb has warned me a couple of times. Then, at the end of the day, I pick Keneil up and rush home to keep an eye on the boys, especially Devon who can be a bit of a handful, till Mum comes home.

Like I said, my mum's got THREE jobs! Some people's mums haven't even got *one*! Like Lissa's mum. When I asked Lissa what her mum did all day she said, 'Nothing. She just goes to Health Watch and Neighbourhood Watch meetings and hair and acupuncture appointments and yoga and Pilates sessions. Oh yeah, and she goes shopping and meets her friends for coffee and lunch.'

She sounds pretty busy to me. My mum doesn't do anything except look after us and clean for people.

Mum's called Comfort. When I told people at

my new school her name Dani said, 'What a great name for a mum!' and everyone laughed. Dani's right: it is. But then she said to me, 'I bet she's lovely. No offence, but with a name like that I imagine her to be big and fat and warm and squashy. Is she?'

'No,' I said. 'Not a bit.' Because she's the opposite. She's skinny and wiry and cool and lively. Only lately she's not been quite as lively as she used to be.

But she's still lovely – and kind and gentle and fun and we love her loads and she's the VERY BEST MUM IN THE WORLD. This morning Devon said he was going to marry her when he grew up and Marlon pointed out you're not allowed to marry your mum so Devon said, 'Yes I can!' and Marlon said, 'No you can't!' so Devon punched him. Then Keneil started crying because he wanted to marry Mum too, but the good thing was I could leave them all to it as it was Saturday and Mum was home to sort it.

It must be quiet in Lissa's house. She's only got one brother. It must be MEGA quiet in Ali and Dani's houses because they've got no brothers at all, just a sister each.

I wish I had a sister. I wish I had a sister like

Alana de Silva. I burn with happiness as it dawns on me that tomorrow I'm going to meet her face to face! I can't wait to tell Mum.

I run across the forecourt in front of the flats and burst through the front doors, narrowly missing some girls on their way out. 'Stuck-up cow!' I hear one of them say, but I don't care. Some people round here make comments about me since I started at Riverside Academy instead of the comp, but they're wrong. I'm not stuck-up and most of the girls at Riverside aren't either.

Optimistically I press the button for the lift. Nine times out of ten it's not working and this is one of those times so I bound up the stairs instead. Good training for netball. I'm captain of Year Seven and we've got some important matches coming up after half term so I need to be fit. I try to make it all the way up to the tenth floor without stopping but it's no good, my heart is bursting. I have to stop for a breather on the eighth. From above I can hear someone crying. There's always some kid howling in our block.

Then I recognize the cry. It's Keneil. I hurry upstairs and bang on our front door but no one answers. From inside I can hear my little brother really going for it. I fish my key out of my pocket and turn it in the lock, but when I push the door something is blocking it. I put my shoulder against it and shove hard, managing to open it wide enough to peek inside. Keneil is sitting with his back against the door, howling miserably.

'Keneil? It's Tasheika.' Keneil stops crying abruptly at the sound of my voice. 'Move, honey. Let me in.'

He scrambles obediently out of the way and I enter the flat. It's a mess. The table is still littered with breakfast debris, there are toys everywhere and crockery is smashed on the floor by the kitchen door. What's been going on? In the corner the television is blaring, but no one is watching it.

I kneel down and give Keneil a hug. He puts his arms round my neck in a stranglehold and starts moaning again. I make soothing noises and pat him better, trying not to squirm as he buries his wet, snotty face in my neck. He smells rank. I glare at Marlon who is huddled on the sofa with his earphones in, wearing the glazed, shut-down look that I know so well.

'Why didn't you take him to the toilet?'

He pulls an earphone out. 'What?'

'He's done it in his pants!'

'I know. It was too late . . . He didn't ask . . .'

'You should be looking after him! Where's Mum?'

I expect him to say, 'Out shopping with Devon,' because there's no sight or sound of my noisy little brother, but instead he points to her bedroom and says, 'Lying down.'

I hitch Keneil up on to my hip and go in search of Mum.

She's lying on the bed with her eyes closed and there's blood everywhere.

Chapter 3

'Mum!' I yell.

Mum's eyes flicker open. 'Tasheika,' she says faintly. Her hand flutters up to her forehead where there is a big open gash. She's also got a black eye and a swollen nose with congealed blood beneath it. Blood is all over the pillow too and the bedspread and on disgusting balls of screwed-up tissue and a towel by the side of the bed.

'What happened?' I say, dumping Keneil on the floor. Immediately he starts grizzling again.

Mum struggles to sit up and fresh blood trickles out of her nostril. She clutches her head. 'Oh dear,' she says, 'my head hurts.'

'What have you done?'

She closes her eyes for a moment then opens them again and stares at me ruefully. 'I walked into a door! How silly was that? I was carrying the dirty breakfast dishes back to the kitchen and I wasn't looking. I walked straight into the corner of it. I didn't half give myself a bang.'

'Mum! You must be more careful! You've really hurt yourself this time!'

'It looks worse than it is,' she says, grabbing the towel to staunch the blood, which is gaining momentum. 'Come here, baby,' she says, reaching out for Keneil, but he backs away from her, hiding behind my legs. I'm not surprised; she looks scary.

'I'll call an ambulance,' I say.

'No! I'm fine.'

'Mum! You need your head stitched up! It looks awful!'

'I'll be all right in a minute.'

'Have you seen yourself?' I thrust her magnifying make-up mirror into her hands and she peers at herself and groans. I seize the advantage.

'I don't care what you say. We're going to the hospital. You don't want it to scar, do you?'

She stares at herself forlornly in the mirror and pulls a face. 'All right! I'll go and have a couple of stitches just to keep you quiet. Talking of which, the boys are being good, bless them.' She nods, wincing as her head hurts, towards the living room where the only sound now is the television.

'That's because Devon's not there,' I say shortly.

'I think I scared the life out of them,' she says. 'All that blood.'

'I bet you did. Come on, let's get you cleaned up.'

'I can do it,' she says. 'I'm not helpless, just careless. Give me a hand up.'

Then, helping her off the bed with her arm round my neck like she's some old lady not my young fit mum, it suddenly dawns on us both at the same time. And we stare at each other in alarm and say exactly the same thing.

'Where is he then?'

Forget about cleaning up my mum or smelly Keneil or the flat. Mum was freaking out far more about where Devon had got to than getting herself sorted. Devon had run off and goodness knows what he'd be up to. He's not allowed out on the estate on his own because, though most people are OK round here, there are some Mum would never want him mixing with. Like she says, Devon is a good kid, but he's a bundle of energy and attracts trouble like a magnet.

'Why didn't you stop him?!' I yell at Marlon, but I know why. He couldn't if he tried.

He shrugs miserably and carries on listening to his iPod. It's like music is his escape. Music and football. When things get tough my pathetic brother blanks everything out by sticking those flaming earphones in.

All right for him. Not all of us can be so lucky. I feel a sudden surge of anger. I'm going to rip them out of his ears and chuck them over the balcony one day. I wish Mum had never bought him that iPod for Christmas. She couldn't afford it anyway; we had to make do with rubbish crackers and cheap Christmas-tree chocolates to pay for it.

No time to think about that now. I slam the front door behind me, ignoring Keneil's protests, and run downstairs, my footsteps echoing loudly through the stairwell. Outside there's no sign of my little brother so I head for the playground but he's not there either. I look around frantically. Where could he have got to?

Then I spot a kid from my old school. 'Have you seen our Devon?' I ask and he points towards the back of the flats by the bins where the older kids hang out. My heart sinks. I run over to the corner, then stop and peer round cautiously. You never know what they might be up to.

There's a gang of kids, six or seven of them, mainly boys and a couple of girls who I recognize immediately as the ones who called me stuck-up. I recognize most of the boys too. They're not doing much, just fooling about and flirting. One of the boys, who's called Ajay, is practising his dance moves and the girls are looking on admiringly.

He's not the only one. I breathe a sigh of relief as I spot Devon on his haunches behind a skip piled high with rubbish, watching him too. They don't even know he's there.

'Devon!' I say in a loud whisper and he spins round. The others glance over and Ajay stops dancing and calls, 'Tasheika! Come and join us, girl.'

But to Devon's disappointment I say, 'No thanks,' because I don't want anything to do with them, even Ajay who seems quite friendly.

'Suit yourself,' says one of the girls sourly and they all turn away, except for Ajay who grins at Devon and says, 'Hey, little bruv,' and Devon smiles back in delight. But you can't trust any of them so I say to him, 'Come on, Mum's looking for you,' and his face changes.

He looks up at me anxiously. 'Is she all right?' he asks.

'She'll be fine.' I stare down at him. 'What did you run off for?'

He hangs his head. 'I didn't like the blood,' he mumbles.

I put my arm round his shoulders and steer my little brother back home, away from the bins and the rubbish and the kids who hang about them like flies.

'Neither did I.' I sigh deeply. 'Never mind. We'll take her to the hospital and make her better.'

Chapter 4

I'm packing my bag the night before school and I'm feeling terrible. I've let Ali down. I never made it to meet her after all. It went right out of my head. I hope she's still talking to me. I didn't see her once over half term, nor anyone else for that matter. It's been a rubbish holiday. I'll be glad to go back to school tomorrow.

It's not my fault. Everything went wrong. Mum ended up having to stay in hospital.

We went there all together in a taxi because Mum wouldn't let me call an ambulance, even though the boys were clamouring for a ride in one. She got herself cleaned up a bit while I dumped Keneil in the bath and dressed him in clean clothes, but she still looked awful and, by the time we got to the hospital, her nose was bleeding again, loads. The taxi driver wasn't very happy, what with her leaking everywhere, Devon and Keneil bouncing up and down on his seats and me with just enough money to pay the fare and none left over for a tip. It was all in change too because I'd raided the tin marked ELECTRICITY which sits on a shelf in the kitchen with the other tins.

Anyway, we waited for ages in Accident and Emergency; it's not like on the telly where you go straight in. The kids started playing up. They were hungry, you see, but there was no money left to buy anything. Marlon just put his earphones in and went quiet, but the other two started racing around and you could tell they were getting on everyone's nerves.

Eventually, Mum's name was called and she wanted to go in on her own but Keneil started to cry, and then she thought she'd better keep an eye on Devon. In the end, we all trooped in to see the doctor with her.

He examined her closely and asked her how it happened and when she said she'd walked into a door he looked like he didn't believe her, even though it was true. Anyway, he sent her for X-rays, so we all went down to the basement of the hospital with Mum in a wheelchair and Keneil on her knee, having a ride.

It turned out she'd broken her nose but they couldn't do much about it. So after they'd stitched up her head, we thought we could go home. But they wouldn't let her go. They said she might have bleeding into the brain and they had to keep her in overnight to monitor her. She did look awful.

She was having none of it but they wouldn't back down. It got a bit embarrassing then, with Mum arguing that she didn't need to stay in and the doctor insisting that she did, and when he wouldn't take no for an answer she was practically shouting at him. Then she got up and said, 'Come on, kids, we're going. NOW!' and suddenly this nurse said, 'Is there no one else besides you to look after the children, Mrs Campbell?' and everything went quiet. You could've heard a pin drop, even though it was only for a few seconds.

Then Mum said scornfully, like the nurse was mad, 'Of course there is. Their father can look after them!' and we all looked at her in surprise. And before we could say anything she went, 'Oh, all right then, just give me a minute to arrange things, *if you don't mind*,' to the doctor and the nurse as if it was all their fault and they nodded and left us in peace, pulling the curtains round us so it was like we were in a little private bedroom of our own.

And Marlon said, 'Are we going to see Dad?' and his face was all excited and hopeful and so was Devon's and even little Keneil's, even though he didn't know who Dad was. But Mum shook her head guiltily and glanced at the curtains, then drew us all towards her.

'I need you to listen carefully,' she whispered. And then she told us her plan.

Chapter 5

First day back. Mum did my beads for me this morning. School colours today: blue and yellow. She threads them through my hair and they look really cool.

Then she turns me round to face her, puts her hands on my shoulders and looks me straight in the eye.

'Now remember, Tasheika,' she says, her face stiff and serious. 'Not a word to anyone at school about what happened. It's our little secret. Promise?'

'I promise.' I knew it was important not to tell – not Dani, not Lissa, not even Ali, even though we'd vowed never to keep a secret from each other.

Ali is waiting at the bus stop, hair in a ponytail, neat as a new pin. I can't help noticing she's tugged her school skirt up, turning the waistband

25

over so it's nice and short, showing off her legs. She didn't do that before half term. Before the fashion show.

'Hi,' I say.

'Hiya,' she says and looks the other way.

'Did you have a nice half term?'

'It was OK,' she says and checks her watch like the most important thing in the world to her is what time the bus is coming.

I take a deep breath. 'I'm really sorry I couldn't come to your house on Sunday,' I begin, even though I'd already said this to her on the phone when I realized what I'd done. My manic Saturday had been followed by an even crazier Sunday as I looked after the boys on my own while Mum was in hospital. All thoughts of meeting Ali had shot right out of my head.

We hadn't talked for long on the phone; she'd said she had to go, her dinner was ready. But she didn't call me back afterwards. She didn't call me back all week, even though I'd left her messages.

''S'all right,' she says like she doesn't care. But she still won't look at me.

'I just forgot,' I say desperately. 'It went clean out of my head.'

She shrugs. 'It doesn't matter.' But it does.

'Something came up, you see,' I say, but she says airily, 'Oh good, the bus is coming,' even though it's miles away.

'Ali, listen –'

'Tash, it's fine.'

'No, it isn't –'

She steps forward, ignoring me, and puts her hand out and, at last, the bus pulls up next to us. I stand behind her on the platform as she pays her fare, then I press my free pass against the machine and follow her to her seat. At least she hasn't sat by someone else. Alice wouldn't, she's not mean. Instead, she stares out of the window, ignoring me.

'I'm really, really sorry,' I say. She bites her lip as I add softly, 'You know how much I wanted to come.'

'Yeah,' she says, her cheeks pink, 'I know how much you wanted to spend time with my famous sister.'

'I wanted to spend time with *you*!' I protest, though it is true I was dying to meet her sister in person.

'So why didn't you then?' She turns to me and for the first time ever I see a flash of anger in her eyes.

I hesitate. I'd promised Mum I wouldn't tell anyone.

'Something important came up,' I repeat feebly and my best friend, the nicest, kindest, gentlest person in the world (except for my mum), finally snaps.

'Well thanks a *bunch*, Tasheika! If you had something more important to do than meet me *as arranged*, then that's fine. But you could at least have had the *decency* to tell me instead of leaving me waiting on the bridge like a lemon *ALL AFTERNOON*!'

I stare at her in shock. I've never heard Ali raise her voice before. Her face has gone from pink to bright red.

She gives an embarrassed little cough. 'Sorry,' she says.

'That's OK, I deserve it.' Then I add curiously, 'How long did you wait?'

'Ages,' she says gruffly. 'An hour and ten minutes.'

'Oh, Ali,' I groan.

'I kept thinking you'd come. So I waited and waited, even though I was freezing.'

'You're so good . . .'

'And then it started raining. I was soaked through.'

28

'I'm sorry!' I bite my lip because I so want to tell her the reason I couldn't come but I'm not allowed.

'My mum told me off when I got home.'

'Oh no! I bet your mum hates me now!' I wait for reassurance otherwise, but she carries on.

'*And* the Barbies went past. They asked me who I was waiting for and when I said you they laughed and said I'd have a long wait!'

'What a cheek!' I splutter, narked at the thought of Georgia, Chantelle and Zadie, three girls from our class who are *so* up themselves, having a laugh at my expense.

'They were right,' she points out reasonably and I say, 'Oh yeah, I suppose they were,' and then we both look at each other and burst out laughing.

When we get off the bus, she says casually, 'I went to tea at Lissa's house during half term.'

'That was nice.' I swallow a bitter lump of jealousy that has settled in my throat. 'Did you have fun?'

'Not as much as fun as I'd have had with you.' She tucks her arm through mine and we stroll into school together. Mates again.

I love Ali. She's so serious and proper but

she always sees the funny side of things in the end.

She's the best friend anyone could ever have. I will NEVER let her down again.

Chapter 6

Mum's plan had worked beautifully, though it threw us all, including me, when she announced to the doctor and nurse that my dad would look after us while she was in hospital. She was so convincing she had me believing her for a second, even though we hadn't seen him in years. But, as soon as the doctor and nurse had left us in private, she'd explained to us very carefully that she had to stay in hospital, she had no choice, and in the meantime I, Tasheika, was to be in charge. BUT NO ONE WAS TO KNOW. If anyone asked, we were to say my dad was looking after us. And she promised she'd be home as soon as she could.

'Boys, you've got to be really, really good for Tash,' she said solemnly. And they all crossed their hearts and hoped to die. 'Who's the boss?'

she asked and the boys said, 'Tasheika!' and she smiled at last. Then she gave us all a hug and a kiss and told us to get a taxi and I could pay the driver out of the tin marked WATER and use what was left to keep going till she came home. And we left quickly before the doctor and nurse came back.

But when I turned round to wave goodbye to her she was crying.

Two days later she was home again. I was soooo glad to see her. The boys had been good, considering. But there was so much to do.

They were hungry ALL the time. No sooner had they finished their breakfast, they wanted something else to eat. Same after lunch. And tea. And they got bored with eating the same things. I can't do meals from scratch like Mum, I can only put things in the oven from the freezer, and we were out of fish fingers and chips and pizza and easy stuff, so we lived on cereal and crisps and beans on toast.

And Keneil kept doing it in his pants, I don't know why. Maybe he had a stomach upset or was just missing Mum. It wasn't his fault, poor thing; he didn't like it.

The first night, he kept waking up asking for

Mum so in the end I brought him into my bed. He was like a wriggly, smelly hot-water bottle. Sunday morning, he woke up early and wanted to play. I was so tired! Both he and Devon were extra wound up all day because the weather was bad and they were stuck inside. Marlon was the complete opposite. He stayed slouched in front of the telly while the other two crashed around the flat. Devon was bored out of his skull and wanted to go out to play but I wouldn't let him.

Sunday night, I was totally knackered. It had been a rotten day. And then I remembered it was supposed to be the day I went to Ali's and I'd forgotten all about it. I phoned her and she wouldn't speak to me, so I cried myself to sleep, my arms wrapped round stinky little Keneil.

When Mum walked in on Monday morning I thought I was going to cry again. Keneil's face lit up like the sun and he rushed into her arms.

'I'm sorry it's a bit of a mess,' I said helplessly. She wrinkled her nose cos Keneil was still a bit whiffy but gave me a big smile.

'Tasheika, my darling, you're a star,' she said. 'I don't know what I'd have done without you.'

That made it all worthwhile. But then she sat Marlon and Devon and me down, not Keneil because he didn't understand, and made us all promise never to tell anyone she'd left us in the flat on our own.

'It's Top-Secret Classified Information, Never to be Disclosed, not even under Threat of Torture!' she said, making a game of it. The boys' eyes sparkled, they love all this cryptic cloak-and-dagger stuff, and I knew they'd never tell a soul. But I felt sick because I knew it wasn't a game.

Mum took over straight away: washing, cleaning, putting the flat to rights. Then we went shopping and when we came home she cooked a proper dinner for us. She did her special jerk chicken recipe with garlic and peppers and onions. It was delicious!

Apart from the fact that her eye was still partially closed and her nose was a bit swollen and she had stitches in her forehead, Mum seemed back to normal. Well, better than normal actually, because, like I said, she hadn't been too good lately. A rest in hospital had done her the world of good. She should've stayed in for longer. But I'm glad she didn't.

She went back to work the next day and I was sort of in charge still for the remainder of half term. But it was different now because Mum was home for lunch and tea and all I had to do was take Keneil to and from nursery and keep an eye on the others while she was at work. We hung out in the park and kicked a football around and did the shopping together and I made sure Devon kept well away from Ajay and his gang.

Now we're back in school again, back to our old routine, and Keneil's stopped pooping his pants. He likes nursery and I LOVE school and Marlon and Devon are doing OK too so far as I know. And Mum's properly in charge again. Cool.

We don't need anyone else. We can manage now we've got our mum back.

Chapter 7

First day back after half term and school settles down. It's like the fashion show never happened. Except now everyone wants to be friends with Ali. They've all seen another side to her since she organized that show practically single-handed. She's *my* best mate, not theirs!

Anyway, the real reason they want to be friends with her is because they've found out that her sister is the amazing Alana de Silva.

You'd never have thought it. Alice Grimes is so quiet and serious she sort of fades into the background unless you know her really well like I do. (Though, obviously, I didn't know her as well as I thought I did!) She's really pretty, with big eyes that sort of sweep upwards at the corners and high cheekbones and nice-shaped lips, but she's not into clothes or fashion like the rest of us (except Dani!).The thing she really cares about is the environment.

But Nikki, her sister, is the complete opposite. It turns out Nikki Grimes is not only Alana de Silva, THE most uber-beautiful model ever (I am her greatest fan), but also one half of THE most glamorous power couple of the moment with her boyfriend, West Park Wanderers striker, Titch Mooney. The press have nicknamed them Aloony de Mooney because Alana has a reputation for being a bit of a hell-raiser. But, like Ali pointed out, it's not really her fault. The fame and lifestyle went to her head at first and she didn't know how to handle it. It wasn't as bad as it seemed though. The media had hyped it up.

I hope I get to meet her sometime. Ali, who never holds a grudge, says of course I can, anytime, but it's not that simple. I'm not like Ali or Dani or Lissa. Apart from school I don't have much – no, I don't have *any* – time to myself.

Mum relies on me, you see. I don't mind, honest I don't. But I wish she'd let me explain to Ali why I couldn't get to meet her that Sunday.

She won't let me though. Mum doesn't want anyone to know we were left on our own when she was in hospital. She said she'd get into trouble if anyone found out. That's why she told them at the hospital that my dad was still around.

She's working today. I hope she's OK.

'Tasheika Campbell, are you paying attention?'

'Yes, Miss.'

Mrs Waters, our PE teacher, doesn't miss a trick.

'Because if we intend to win this series of matches we all have to give one hundred per cent.'

'Yes, Miss.'

'Especially you, because you're captain.'

'Yes, Miss.'

'So that means practices every lunchtime . . .'

As Mrs Waters' voice drones on, I breathe a huge sigh of relief. I was so afraid they'd be after school like last half term. I missed a couple of practices because I had to pick up Keneil from the nursery and I lied and said I had dental appointments. Worse still, once I was playing in an important match and it was running late so I had to come off the court to go and get him. I pretended I was feeling ill.

'Keep our arrangements to yourself, Tasheika,' Mum had warned me.

I'd got away with it with Mrs Waters but I

knew my friends didn't believe me. Especially Lissa. Winning is everything to her. She'd carry on playing if she was at death's door.

She thinks she'd make a better captain than me, I know she does. She would too. She's *sooo* dependable.

I'm dependable too! At home my mum depends on me loads. But they don't know this at school because she's made me promise not to tell anyone. 'It's our secret,' she says.

'I will pin the netball fixtures on the noticeboard,' continues our teacher. 'The matches will take place on Thursdays after school: some home, some away. You will need to check the board for dates and alterations.'

I find myself beaming from ear to ear. This must be my lucky day! Mum's three jobs mean that during the week she cleans the Staffy Arms every morning, offices in town every evening and in the afternoons she goes to different private houses. Except Thursdays! Thursday afternoon is her afternoon off!

Perfect! She can pick up Keneil and be there for the boys and I can play in the netball matches. I'll just have to make sure I'm home in time for her to go to work at night.

'What are you looking so pleased about?' asks Dani.

'Looking forward to leading my team to victory,' I say and Dani nods approvingly. I feel like jumping up and down with happiness like Keneil does. But then, out of the corner of my eye, I catch her exchanging a fleeting look with Lissa.

They think I'm going to let them down again.

Well, I'm not going to. I'll show them.

Tasheika Campbell is going to be the most reliable netball captain Riverside Academy has ever seen!

Chapter 8

We've got private study in the library instead of
French because Madame Dupré's away. It's really
quiet with everyone reading or doing their prep.
I like it in here, it's peaceful, not like home. I'm
giving Ali a hand with her English because I've
finished mine. She struggles a bit with English and
maths, though she's really good at science and
geography.

It's vocab. Matching words with their definitions.
I love words. I love their sounds and meanings
and the way every day someone comes up with
a new word and then it becomes part of our
language. I'd love to make up a new word.

Miss Webb, our fab form teacher and the best
English teacher ever, says I should be an etymologist
when I grow up. An etymologist is someone who
studies how words evolve. It sounds interesting.

But I'd rather be a top model like Alana de Silva.

I'm lucky, me. I'm good at everything. I'm not boasting – it's true. That's probably why I won a full academic scholarship to Riverside Academy. They award one every year. Mum doesn't have to pay for a thing, except uniform and trips and things like that. We've got a tin marked SCHOOL for that sort of stuff. We've got a tin for everything in our house; Mum's very organized. So am I, except when things go wrong.

'Reticent?' whispers Ali. I glance down the list of definitions and point to '*Reserved, uncommunicative, inclined to secrecy*'.

'Thanks!'

Oh dear. I'm *inclined to secrecy*. But not from choice. I'm definitely not *reserved* or *uncommunicative* though. I sigh deeply into the silence of the library and Dani looks up. She crosses her eyes with boredom and sticks her tongue out of the side of her mouth. I suppress a giggle. She is sooooo funny.

Dani's got a scholarship too, but hers is for sport. She's fantastic. She's the captain of the hockey team and she'd probably be captain of the netball team too, only Mrs Waters said she couldn't be both so everyone chose me instead. Lissa was disappointed; you could tell she was hoping they'd choose her. Dani spends her weekends playing football with boys. She looks like a boy herself with her short hair and cheeky face.

Everyone has to pass a test to get into Riverside but some people still have to pay. Lissa's parents pay for her to come here. They can afford it. She's frowning over her book but she won't ask for help.

Dani grins at me then deliberately nudges her with her elbow. Lissa looks up annoyed, then sees Dani laughing at her and nudges her back harder.

'Melissa Hamilton? What do you think you're doing?' intones the teacher on duty. 'Don't disturb Danielle when she's trying to work.'

Lissa's jaw drops open with the injustice of it but she won't snitch on a friend. I smile to myself then turn my attention back to Ali, pointing out a mistake she's made. She rubs it out gratefully and tries again.

I think Ali's parents pay something towards the fees too but not all of it. They're not rich like Lissa's. Ali says Lissa's house is amazing, like something out of a magazine.

On our table in the library are the girls we call the Barbies: Georgia, Chantelle and Zadie. Their parents must've spent a fortune getting them into

43

Riverside because they only share one brain cell between them and that belongs to Georgia. Ali's a bit in awe of them because they try to make out they're more sophisticated than us, but, personally, I think they're pathetic. The others do exactly what Georgia says. They even copy the way she does her hair.

Not like us! Ali and Lissa and Dani couldn't do their hair like mine if they tried. Mine's thick and wiry with bright shiny beads in it, Lissa's is long and silky with expensive clasps, Dani's is short and spiky like a boy's, and Ali's is scraped back off her face in a no-nonsense ponytail. We're not a bit alike to look at. We're not a bit alike personality-wise either. But we get on really well. Mrs Waters called us the Gang of Four, but since the morning after the fashion show we've decided to call ourselves the No Secrets Club instead.

I wriggle uncomfortably in my seat. I shouldn't really be part of this club. I *have* got a secret. They'll chuck me out if they discover it!

At that very moment Ali looks up at me and bizarrely I think, *Oh no! She knows!* But, instead, she snaps her book shut and smiles at me gratefully.

'Finished!' she whispers. 'Thanks for your help.'

I smile back happily. Mum's home now, it's all over and there's nothing to worry about any more. No one need ever find out. The bell's about to go for lunch and my world is back to rights. Time to grab a quick sandwich with my three best mates then spend half an hour on the netball court.

I LOVE school.

Because the sun's shining we make for our favourite spot, the picnic tables near the courts, even though it's nearly November and the clocks have gone back. I'm entitled to a free lunch but I'd rather have a packed one with my friends. Today I've made a sandwich using the remains of the salt beef we had for Sunday dinner with pickle and peppers. It's yummy. Lissa is complaining as usual.

'Brie and cranberry baguette,' she says, turning her nose up even though it looks delicious, all wrapped up cosily in a red serviette with delicate baby spinach leaves peeking out. 'I've told my mum I don't like Brie but she never listens.'

'Make your sandwiches yourself,' I say. 'Then you can have what you want.'

'Like me!' mumbles Dani, her mouth full of flaky pastry, but she doesn't really make her own lunch. Her mum's a nurse and she gives Dani money every day to buy what she wants on the way to school. Today she's bought three sausage rolls. I'm not that lucky. I use up whatever I can find in the fridge. But at least I get to choose.

Lissa eyes the remaining sausage rolls enviously. 'Swap you half a baguette for one of those?'

Dani shrugs. 'Take them both if you want, I'm stuffed. They're really filling.'

Lissa grabs them quickly before Dani can change her mind. When she's finished them she eats up the other half of the baguette and then trades her organic natural yoghurt for one of Ali's chocolate brownies. Lissa's lunchbox is an advert for healthy eating, but she's always hungry and she's got a really sweet tooth so she's forever scrounging food or swapping the contents of her lunchbox with us. She never puts on weight though. She's thin as a rake.

'Come on!' I say, washing my sandwich down with a bottle of water I've filled from the tap. 'We don't want to be late for practice.'

'Have fun,' says Ali, looking wistful. Poor Ali. She didn't make it into the netball team, not even the squad, though she's not that bad. She just lacks confidence, that's all.

'Come and watch us!' I say, but as we get up to go the Barbies sidle over.

'Hi, Alice. Mind if we join you?' Georgia's voice is high and wheedling like she's afraid Ali will say no. Ali wouldn't do that, she's too polite.

The irony is (I feel quite proud of myself using the word 'irony' correctly: Miss Webb taught us it means *the opposite of what you expect*) for the first half term Georgia thought Ali was the most boring person who had ever walked the planet. But that's all changed now.

By the time the practice is over, Ali is surrounded by half of Year Seven.

Everyone wants to be best friends with Alana de Silva's sister.

Chapter 9

Ali invites Lissa to her house for tea on Wednesday.

'You can come too!' says Ali when she sees my face, but I can't. I've got to pick Keneil up from nursery.

'Come on Thursday then, after practice,' says Ali. But I can't do that either. Even though it's Mum's afternoon off, she still has her evening job. I'm not allowed to tell anyone that either because you're not supposed to leave children under a certain age alone in a house at night without a responsible adult in charge.

'You're more responsible than any adult I know,' Mum said to me when she first got her evening job. 'But that's the law so we'll just keep it our little secret, yeah?'

Another secret! Well, I guess it's the same one really. On the whole our system works well. Mum comes home from work, gives us our tea, puts Keneil to bed and goes out to work again. We wash up and I listen to Devon read while Marlon does his homework and then the boys watch telly while I do mine. That's the rule. Plus we're not allowed to answer the door to anyone. By the time we're ready for bed Mum is home again. Simple. What's the problem?

I think the people who make the laws in this country, the MPs and that, can't have any children. Or they're all men and their wives are posh like Lissa's mum and go to Pilates and yoga and have their nails done and are back home before their children come out of school. Because if MPs were single mums like mine with three different jobs they'd have to change the law to allow their kids to look after themselves while they were out at work.

I said this to Mum and she said, 'Maybe I should become an MP then. If I had an MP's salary I wouldn't need three jobs. And I could have a babysitter on expenses!'

'Why don't you, Mum?' I say in excitement. 'You could be prime minister!'

She laughed. 'Good idea! I could make all the rules!' Then she added, 'Tell you what, Tash

49

love, you work hard at school and pass all your exams and *you* could be prime minister one day.'

Perhaps I won't be a famous supermodel like Alana de Silva after all. Maybe I'll be prime minister instead and make my mum proud of me.

On Wednesday, when Lissa goes to Ali's house for tea, I catch the bus home with them. It's a later one than usual because normally I dash straight off, but Lissa faffs about and we miss it. It's OK, I won't be late for Keneil. I'm not jealous any more because Ali explained to me in the toilets this morning that her mum said she had to ask Lissa to tea because she'd been to hers over half term.

'You can come another time,' she'd said and I promised I would. I was determined to. I'd have a word with Mum and see if we could sort something out. 'I'd much rather it was you,' she added and I believed her. Then Lissa walked in and we had to stop talking. She looked at us funny as if she knew we'd been talking about her but she didn't say anything.

We sit at the back of the bus playing a silly game together, one I made up. You take it in turns to say you'll marry the next bloke that gets on the bus. It's really funny.

'Me first!' bags Lissa, but then she changes her mind when she gets a kid with a squint and a snotty nose.

'He doesn't count, he's too young!' she protests, but we both say, 'Yes he does!' and we're all laughing at this poor kid so much his mum gives us a dirty look. Then Ali goes next and gets an old man, bald with no teeth, and now we're practically rolling in the aisle. Then it's my turn, but for the next two stops only women get on.

'You can marry women now,' Ali points out helpfully, but this makes us laugh even more so we decide to stick with men. When the bus pulls in at the next stop Lissa looks out of the window and says, 'OMG! You should see yours!' and I know she's taking the mickey and it's going to be someone really weird so I'm afraid to look. I curl up on the back seat with my hands over my face, groaning theatrically.

But when I peep through my fingers I can see the outline of a boy in school uniform, showing his pass to the driver.

'*He* is gorgeous!' breathes Lissa.

'He is, Tash!' whispers Ali. So, as the boy walks up the aisle towards us I lower my hands to have a proper look. His eyes meet mine and he smiles.

'Hi, Tasheika.'

It's Ajay. He looks different in school uniform. Beside me I hear a sharp intake of breath. In stereo.

'Hiya,' I say, wondering why I'd never noticed before just how good-looking he is. Maybe because up to now I'd only ever seen him hidden inside a hoody. For a minute I think he's actually going to sit beside me and my heart practically stops. But his eyes shift to the others and at the last moment he folds himself into the seat in front of us, inserts his earphones and retreats into a world of his own. Like Marlon does. It must be a male thing.

Beside me my friends' eyes are popping out of their heads. '*Who's he?*' Lissa mouths at me but I ignore her and stare out of the window.

He gets off at the stop before ours, where the shops are. Then the questions come thick and fast:

Who is he?

What's his name?

How old is he?

How do you know him?

Has he got a girlfriend?

This last one is from Lissa. I hope she's not

turning into a Barbie. But I just say honestly, 'His name's Ajay. I don't know him that well. He lives near me.'

'I wish he lived near me!' says Lissa enviously.

'He goes to the same school as Austen,' says Ali. 'I recognize the uniform.' Austen Penberthy is Ali's friend from primary school. Her friend, NOT her boyfriend, as she's always reminding us.

We get off by the bridge on Ali's side. Just as I'm about to say goodbye and run across it, Lissa says, 'Look at that lot!' On the other side of the bypass, my side, someone has set fire to a bin and a load of kids are pulling burning debris from it and chucking it at each other.

'Hooligans!' she says.

I freeze. One of them, a kid in a red anorak, is Devon. I stare transfixed as my little brother whirls a long piece of rope round his head, in a world of his own, watching the sparks fly off the fraying ends. He's so absorbed in what he's doing that he hasn't even noticed me.

'Look at them!' repeats Lissa. 'They are, literally, playing with fire.'

'They're just kids,' says Ali.

'Precisely!' says Lissa. 'Oi, you lot!' she shouts. 'What do you think you're doing?'

Devon glances up and sees me and drops the rope as if he's been burned. The ringleader, who I recognize as Mason Riley, a bit older than Devon and seriously bad news, gives her a mouthful of abuse and the others laugh, all except Devon. Lissa is shocked.

'Honestly!' she gasps. 'You wonder what sort of families these kids come from.' She sounds just like her mother.

'They're off the estate,' says Ali and I flinch. No sooner are the words out of her mouth than her face turns pink. 'Sorry! I don't mean . . . I didn't mean . . .'

'Got to go!' I say flatly and leg it over the bridge. The kids on the other side scatter in all directions as they see me coming and the one who runs away from me fastest of all is my own brother. But I'm not chasing him. I just want to get away from Lissa and her patronizing voice.

And Ali. She's just as bad.

Chapter 10

When I get to the nursery I'm all hot and bothered and out of sorts. Who do Lissa and Ali think they are?

'Been a good boy today?' I ask my baby brother and Keneil rewards me with a big beaming grin and tucks his warm little hand into mine.

'He's always a good boy, aren't you, Keneil?' My little brother nods righteously as Jo, the nursery assistant, hands me his bag. She's already buttoned him into his coat, just to make the point that I'm a teeny bit late.

I'm glad one of you is, I think crossly to myself. *You wait till I get my hands on your brother. Brothers! Marlon knows he's not supposed to let Devon out of his sight till I get home.*

'Can you remember to bring his apron for art

tomorrow?' says Jo. 'And a warm hat for outdoor play.'

'Anything else?' I say a bit shirtily. Is she having a go at me?

'You forgot to sign his diary yesterday,' she reminds me and I feel a surge of impatience. That's Mum's job, not mine, though I'm not going to point it out to her.

'We're rubbish, aren't we, Kenny?' I say and he giggles.

'Rubbish!' he echoes. 'Put us in the bin!'

Out of the mouths of babes and innocents! Put us in the bin! That's just what people like Lissa and her mum would like to do. And Ali. And Jo probably.

She smiles at him affectionately and ruffles his hair. 'Can't put you in the bin! I want to see you tomorrow.' He grins happily and then I feel bad. She's all right, Jo. It's not her fault I'm feeling like this.

I wonder where Devon's got to but I'm not too worried. He'll have scarpered off home, knowing he's in trouble. My phone is ringing. It's Ali. I ignore it.

Keneil and I walk home together hand in hand singing 'The Wheels on the Bus', his favourite song, at the tops of our voices. He doesn't complain about how far it is if we sing. We go through every single verse, each one practically identical:

The mums on the bus go chat, chat, chat . . .
The wipers on the bus go swish, swish, swish . . .
The grannies on the bus go knit, knit, knit . . .

He knows them all off by heart and won't let me leave out a single one – not dads, not children, not babies, none of them. 'More!' he demands in his imperious little voice and, I'm not kidding, it starts to get really boring. In the end, even he gets fed up and starts to whinge that he wants to be picked up. But he's really heavy now and I've got too much to carry so, to keep him going on the last haul, I make up a special new verse for him about a boy on the bus.

It goes like this:

The boy on the bus goes smile, smile, smile,
Smile, smile, smile,
Smile, smile, smile,
The boy on the bus he makes me smile,
All day long.

He likes it. He makes me sing it again. And again. 'Louder!' he roars. 'Louder!'

So there I am, walking along the street leading to the flats, hand in hand with a bossy three-year-old, belting out a song I've just made up at the top of my voice over and over again, when suddenly I get the feeling someone is walking behind me.

I spin round and there he is.

Ajay.

Shirt out, tie at half-mast, bag on shoulder, munching on a bar of chocolate. Oh yes, and grinning from ear to ear.

I want to die. I turn back again and keep on walking, silent now. 'Sing it again,' orders Keneil. I wish he'd shut up.

Ajay falls into step beside me but I keep looking firmly ahead. I can feel Keneil staring up at him. 'What's this one called then?' asks Ajay.

'Keneil.'

'Hey, Keneil, want some chocolate?'

My little brother stops and falls instantly in love with Ajay as he bends down beside him and breaks him off a bit.

'Take some more,' says Ajay, and Keneil obliges, his eyes shining.

'That's enough!' I say and it comes out a bit sharp. 'You won't eat your tea.'

'Do as your sister says, little bruv. Keep it for later.'

He stands up and offers me some but I'm too embarrassed to take it. I feel really, really stupid, him catching me like that, singing a song I'd made up about him! He must think I fancy him!

'Where've your friends gone?'

'Home. They don't live round here.'

'Thought not.' He looks at my school uniform. 'You go to that posh girls' school, don't you?'

I nod. What else can you say?

'What's it like?'

'Good.'

He studies me thoughtfully. His eyes are dark with long thick lashes. I look away quickly. Tasheika Campbell, lost for words. My friends wouldn't recognize me.

'What they called?'

'Who?'

'Your friends.' *What is he, a mind-reader? Hope not!*

'Lissa's the one with long hair and Ali's the one with the ponytail.' I wonder which one he's interested in. Then I can't resist adding, 'Ali's sister is Alana de Silva.'

'What? The one off the telly?' He looks impressed. 'The one who goes out with Titch Mooney?'

I nod and he says, 'Respect!'

That's it, I think with a pang. He'll like Ali more than me now.

He would anyway. I mean, let's face it, what bloke would ever want to get know a girl who's always got kids in tow. I feel myself coming over all moody as he adds, 'Your brother's a good footballer for his age.'

'What?'

'Marlon.' He nods over at the front of the flats where coats and bags are laid out on the ground as goalposts and a gang of kids are kicking a ball around. 'He's your brother, yeah?'

I spot him straight away, running around with his arms in the air, happy as Larry cos he's just scored a goal. Little monkey! No wonder Devon was running riot with that Mason Riley. Marlon was supposed to be in the flat keeping an eye on him!

'Marlon!' I yell. 'Inside! Now!'

Chapter 11

The lift's not working again. Marlon dashes up the stairs as fast as he can, knowing he's about to get it in the neck from me. By the time I've hauled Keneil and bags up ten flights of steps he and Devon are sitting side by side on the sofa innocently watching telly like butter wouldn't melt in their mouths. I switch it off and eyeball them both, hands on hips.

'Why weren't you looking after him, Marlon?' I demand.

'I was right outside. I knew where he was!' he says defensively.

'Oh yeah? And where would that be?'

'In here, watching telly!'

'Wrong!' I glare at Devon this time. 'Tell him where you were, Devon!'

Devon mumbles something inaudible.

'He was playing on the bypass,' I say, stretching the point a bit, 'with a gang of kids. They'd set a bin alight!'

'It wasn't me!' says Devon automatically. 'Mason Riley did it!'

'You shouldn't be hanging round with Mason Riley, you know that! You shouldn't have been outside in the first place. I'm telling Mum!'

'Ohhhhh!' Devon's bottom lip comes out and he folds his arms and flings himself backwards on the sofa. Marlon looks stricken. He knows he's going to get it too when Mum hears about this.

'That's all she asks you to do: watch out for him till I get home,' I complain, determined to resist the appeal in Marlon's large, soulful eyes. I can't help feeling sorry for him because he hasn't actually done anything wrong, he never does. It's Devon who's trouble on legs. But Marlon's got to start pulling his weight in this family like I do.

I could be round at Ali's now, having tea with the amazing Alana de Silva. But I can't because I've got to pick up Keneil from nursery and keep an eye on everything here till Mum comes home. So Lissa's there instead, having all the fun. Lissa, with her posh house and expensive hair clips and healthy lunchbox and a mum who runs around after her all the time.

It's not fair.

'I'm hungry,' says Keneil and to everyone's surprise, including mine, I snap. I should've said comfortingly, 'Mum will be home soon, babe,' and fetched him a carrot stick. Instead I shout, 'Tough!' and walk into my bedroom and slam the door.

And I don't come out till I hear Mum's voice.

'Hello, boys. Where's Tasheika?' she says and I shoot up from my bed where I'd been lying for the past half hour staring blankly at the ceiling, feeling sorry for myself. I'd ignored the others in the living room while I wallowed in self-pity, imagining the fantastic time Lissa was having at *my* best friend's house talking to *my* idol. Unsurprisingly, they'd left me alone.

I'd thought about Ajay too and how different he'd seemed in his school uniform and to my surprise I'd found myself wishing I hadn't had to cut short the conversation I was having with him to sort out my brothers. Story of my life! Everything – school, netball, friends – comes second to looking after them.

And then I'd got cross with myself because I didn't even like him anyway! Until today I'd thought of him as someone to avoid.

In the end I didn't know what to think. I felt completely out of sorts, all churned-up inside, not a bit like me. So I was really glad Mum was home to take control.

I open my bedroom door and peep out. She's taking her coat off and she spots me and smiles. 'Hi, Tash. Been doing your homework?'

I nod, even though it's a lie. The boys are on the sofa watching CBeebies. Keneil is in the middle, surrounded by bits of chewed-up carrot.

'What have you been eating?' Mum laughs and drops to her knees to give him a kiss. He puts his chubby little arms round her neck and hugs her tight.

'I got it for him,' says Devon. 'He was hungry. But I didn't peel it cos I'm not allowed to use the knife.'

'Good boy,' says Mum and his face lights up into a big pleased smile. He doesn't get a lot of praise. Then he looks at me and his expression becomes wary because he's afraid I'm about to split on him and he'll be back in trouble again. But then something weird happens.

Mum tries to get up but she can't. Her face goes blank and it's like she's forgotten how to get to her feet.

'Give us a hand, Tash,' she says, so I pull her up but her leg is folding beneath her like it's got a mind of its own. Mum sits down heavily on the sofa, right on top of Marlon who yelps and wriggles over to make room, and rubs her thigh hard. 'Flipping leg, it's gone to sleep. Been like this all day. It feels like I've trapped a nerve or something.' She puts her head back and sighs heavily. 'I'm so flaming tired, I don't know what's the matter with me. I wish I didn't have to go back out to work tonight.'

At least I think that's what she says because her words come out a bit slurred.

'Stay home!' says Marlon, sitting upright, and she laughs ruefully.

'I wish! I'd better get the tea on.' But she makes no effort to get up. She looks exhausted, leaning back against the sofa, eyes closed. There are dark circles beneath them.

'We'll do it,' I say, feeling bad that I've been so grumpy. 'You put your feet up. Come on, boys.'

And in a line my three little brothers follow me out to the kitchen without a word of complaint because they're good boys really. Mum does as she's told and puts her feet up. But I can't help noticing she has to lift her lazy leg up on to the sofa using her hands because it won't do it on its own.

Chapter 12

Ali says Lissa likes Ajay!

I knew she did! It's obvious. She keeps dropping enormous hints about the four of us hanging out together at the weekend.

'We could all come over to your place on Saturday, if you like,' she says, her face the picture of innocence. 'For a change.'

Yeah, right. I know what her game is. She wants to see Ajay. Well, tough, Lissa. It's Ali he's interested in, not you.

I don't want my friends coming over to mine anyway. They've never been and the flat's a mess. It needs a really good clean up because Mum hasn't been able to do anything with her bad leg.

'I'm busy Saturday.'

'Me too,' says Dani.

'Sunday, then?'

I hesitate. Church. Sunday roast. Maybe in the afternoon I could squeeze in seeing my friends too. But . . . do I want Lissa hanging round the estate, seeing where I live, making comments?

'I can't. I'm busy Sunday too.'

'You're always busy,' she says sourly. 'And, Dani, *you're* just as bad!' She turns her back on us and thrusts her arm through Ali's. 'Looks like it's just you and me hanging out together again, babe,' she says to her.

Dani pulls a face at her behind her back. She doesn't care if we don't fall in with Lissa's plans. Nothing worries Dani.

It worries *me* though. It means Lissa will be spending more time alone with Ali. And though we're all part of the No Secrets Club (if they only knew!) and we've all become really good mates, it's Ali who's really special to me. And, I have to say, that's got nothing whatsoever to do with her being Alana de Silva's sister. We've been best friends since Day One at Riverside Academy.

I *need* Ali. Nobody knows that because, to look at us, I'm the one who's boss and she sort of follows me around. But Ali is really important to me. She's gentle and caring and she's always there. She doesn't know this but when things are

68

getting on top of me at home, I come to school all hot and bothered and sit down next to quiet, still, sensible Alice and straight away I feel myself calming down.

Then I can cope again.

One day I'm going to take Ali home with me to meet everyone. Not yet though. Not till Mum gets better.

Netball training has begun in earnest. We scoff our lunch quickly so we can all get outside. Actually, I ate most of mine in science and I nearly got caught. Miss Riddle asked me a question and I'd just taken a mouthful of fish-paste sandwich (I don't even like fish-paste but there wasn't much else in the cupboard this morning) so I had to stare at her blankly and pretend I didn't know the answer even though I did. It was so annoying, especially when Lissa put her hand up and answered it correctly instead.

I finish off with an apple well past its sell-by date, all soft and floury – yuck! Not the most satisfying lunch. Opposite me, Lissa is munching away happily on one of her mum's homemade apricot flapjacks. She sees me watching her and offers me a piece.

'No thanks,' I say shortly. 'Get a move on!' And she stuffs it all into her mouth obligingly and gets to her feet. I feel mean then. What is it with me? Lissa's my friend, not my enemy.

I run on to the court feeling rotten, but as soon as we start playing I forget all about Mum and home and Lissa and Ali and Ajay (*Ajay? Where did that come from?*) and concentrate on the game. I have to because Mrs Waters is trying me out as Centre today so I'm immediately in the thick of it. I get to play all over the court, helping to get the ball to the Goal Shooter and the Goal Attack. Today Dani's our shooter (she's brilliant!) and Lissa's the Goal Attack.

We're playing against the Year Eights today for the first time and we expect to be made into mincemeat. But straight away it becomes obvious that we're more than a match for our opponents, even if they are older and bigger than us. (In Dani's case, much bigger! Nobody expects her to be good because she's so short.) She's like me though, she's really quick and can jump high too, and soon Year Seven have knocked the stuffing out of Year Eight mainly because (and I'm not boasting, it's true!) I keep intercepting the ball and passing it to Dani or Lissa and they keep popping it into the net! Easy! The others hardly have to do a thing.

I love, love, LOVE netball. There's nothing like seeing the ball coming towards your opponent and jumping in at the last second to snatch it from them. It's an amazing feeling flying through the air and feeling the thud of the ball and your fingers wrapping round it. Then a quick pass and the satisfying swoosh of the net as my mates leap up and place it safely inside. I want this game to go on forever.

At last, Mrs Waters blows her whistle and a huge cheer goes up from the crowd who've gathered to watch us on the other side of the wire. I never even noticed them while I was playing!

'Well played, Year Sevens!' she says, beaming at us. 'Especially you three: Dani, Lissa and Tash. What a team!'

Off court I can see Ali jumping up and down, beside herself with excitement. Dani and Lissa and I grin and high-five each other as the rest of the team hang off our necks.

I'm so glad I came to Riverside Academy! It is TOTALLY, TOTALLY MAGIC!

Chapter 13

I can't wait to tell Mum how good I was in netball. I've been dancing on a cloud all afternoon, beside myself with pride. It's OK to feel proud of yourself if you know you've done well, isn't it?

Grumpy Griffiths, our ancient maths teacher, tells me off. 'Keep still, Miss Campbell!' he grumbles in his gravelly voice. 'You're wriggling about like a worm on a fishing line.'

'Good simile, Sir,' I say approvingly.

'What?' he barks and everyone falls silent. I can feel Ali shrinking into her seat beside me. Most people are scared stiff of Grumpy Griffiths but I'm not. His bark is worse than his bite. He's like one of those big fierce-looking dogs that are actually pretty mellow beneath their ugly exterior. That's a simile too. Not that I'm saying Grumpy Griffiths is ugly.

OK, to be honest, he is a bit. Well, a lot, actually. Unless grey droopy moustaches, beetling eyebrows, tombstone teeth and big warty noses with hairy nostrils is your thing. But like Mum says, you shouldn't judge by appearances.

'A simile,' I explain helpfully, because it's suddenly occurred to me he may not know about them because he's a maths teacher, 'is when you compare two things because they're similar in some way and you use the words "as" or "like". You compared me to a worm on a fishing line because I was wriggling. That's very clever. We did similes with Miss Webb. And metaphors. A metaphor is a direct comparison, omitting the words "as" or "like" –'

'I know what a metaphor is,' he interrupts and now it's so quiet you could hear a pin drop. Ali has totally wilted and has practically disappeared beneath the desk.

Then he adds, 'Tasheika Campbell, you are a mine of information.'

'Thank you, Sir,' I say, flattered.

'A fount of all knowledge.'

'Gosh!'

'An ocean of enlightenment.'

I stare at him in surprise.

'A library of learning . . . A river of expertise . . .'

'Crikey!' Now I'm starting to get worried as he continues to shower me with flowery compliments in front of everyone. I mean, everybody says he's got a soft spot for me but he doesn't have to make it quite so obvious. This is embarrassing; people are starting to giggle.

'A forest of perception . . . A theatre of culture . . . A school of instruction . . . A Wikipedia of data . . .'

Now the class is laughing out loud as our maths teacher declares his admiration for me to the world. I wish he would stop. I'm not sure it's allowed.

Even Ali is in stitches. I turn to her furiously. 'It's not funny!'

'Yes it is!' she splutters. 'You should see your face!'

Finally he comes to a stop and takes a bow and the whole class starts clapping.

'What's going on?' I ask Ali, bewildered.

Dani's voice pipes up from behind me. 'Metaphors,' she explains and understanding dawns on me. Everyone laughs, including Grumpy Griffiths, and a warm feeling floods through me, but it's not embarrassment this time, it's happiness.

I love it here at Riverside Academy.

I love my friends, I love my whole class, I love netball. I even love Grumpy Griffiths.

I am *sooooo* lucky.

The door opens and Mrs Shepherd, our headmistress, appears. The whole class falls silent. Is she going to tell us off for making a noise? Even our teacher looks surprised.

'Excuse me, Mr Griffiths,' she says, her eyes searching the room, 'I'm looking for . . .' Her eyes come to rest on me. 'Tasheika Campbell. Come with me please, Tasheika. Bring your things with you.'

Chapter 14

What have I done?

I get up and sweep everything from my desk into my bag. Ali hands me my lunch bag, eyes wide with concern. My skin is prickly all over like I've fallen into a clump of nettles but I feel cold.

'What's up?' I hear Dani whisper as I walk out of the room. I can feel everyone's eyes on me. Murmurings. An undercurrent of excitement.

'Is she in trouble?' Georgia's voice, clear as a bell.

'Silence!' intones Grumpy Griffiths. 'Back to work, 7LW!'

Mrs Shepherd must've heard what Georgia said because she stops outside the door and turns to face me. 'Don't worry, my dear, you're not in trouble,' she says and her eyes are kind but serious and this makes me worry even more.

'It's your mother,' she continues. 'She's had a bit of an accident.'

My hand flies to my mouth.

Immediately the headteacher drops to her haunches, takes my hands in hers like I'm a little kid and looks me straight in the eye. 'It's all right!' she says. 'She's fine. I had a call from her employer. She collapsed at work this afternoon and she's been taken to West Park Hospital to be checked over. I don't think she's broken anything; it's just a precaution. There's nothing to be alarmed about.'

I believe her, but she's wrong. Even if Mum hasn't hurt herself badly she'll be kept in again, I know she will. It's starting all over again.

I bite my lip, determined not to cry. *Remember what Mum said. Keep it a secret. You can cope, you know you can. You've done it before.*

'Miss Webb is going to drive you to the hospital. You'll feel better when you've seen your mother. Can we get hold of your father, Tasheika?'

'He's at work,' I say quickly, because this time I know what to say. 'I'll phone him later.'

'That's fine.' Mrs Shepherd gets to her feet, looking relieved. 'Off you go, Miss Webb is waiting for you.'

I look up and see Miss Webb, my form teacher, at the end of the corridor and walk towards her. She smiles and says, 'Don't worry, Tash, everything will be all right,' and I smile back weakly and follow her to her car. It's one of those cool Minis with go-faster stripes and normally I would be ecstatic about driving around in it with my favourite teacher. But today I've got other things on my mind.

I sit in silence staring blankly out of the window as Miss Webb pulls out on to the main road. Thoughts are racing round my brain like cars on a racetrack and it's hard to stop them crashing into each other.

You've got to pick up Keneil . . . Has anyone told the nursery you're going to be late? . . . You need to go shopping for tea . . . The boys will be hungry . . . They're always hungry . . . Mum won't be bringing anything home with her today . . . Mum won't be coming home at all . . . How will you manage? . . . You'll need to get something for lunch tomorrow . . . There's nothing there for sandwiches. We've even run out of fish paste . . . The boys'll be OK, they'll have a free school meal . . . You could have a free school meal? . . . NO! Don't want one! . . . Everyone will think I'm rubbish . . . Lissa thinks I'm rubbish already . . . No she doesn't! . . . Mum? . . . I want my mum . . .

A tear trickles down my cheek and I dash it away furiously. We've stopped at traffic lights. Miss Webb is looking at me, concerned. 'Don't worry,' she repeats, 'your mum's going to be fine.' Why is it that the more people tell you not to worry, the more you do? I try to smile but I don't think it comes out right because Miss Webb looks sad, like she doesn't know what else to say. So she pats my knee instead and then, as the car behind us sounds its horn because the lights have changed, she gets in a flummox and the car lurches forward and stalls.

When we get to the hospital the car park is full and there's a queue of cars waiting. Miss Webb growls under her breath and swings the steering wheel round to drive up to the main door instead. 'I'll drop you off at Accident and Emergency, save you waiting,' she says. 'You pop in and find your mum and I'll be there as soon as I can.'

Inside it's really busy. I go up to the desk and give my name and the receptionist says, 'Take a seat, your mother is with the doctor now.'

I do as I'm told and sit down in the crowded waiting room between an old man muttering to himself and a woman with a crying baby. I keep watching the little curtained-off cubicles, trying to work out which one my mum is in. Doctors whisk in and out with files crammed full of notes, while nurses pass to and fro carrying bowls, dressings and water, or dragging big machines behind them.

At last, a guy in a white coat with a stethoscope round his neck comes out of a cubicle and goes up to the desk. I hear him say, 'I want to admit Comfort Campbell for observation. Is there a bed on Holgate?'

My heart sinks, then I jump off my seat and nip into the cubicle quickly before anyone spots what I'm doing. Mum is lying on top of the bed, fully dressed, her head back against the pillows. No blood this time, she looks normal, just worn out and worried. Though I can still see the cut on her forehead which needed stitches.

'Tash!' she says and her face lights up.

'Mum!' I fling myself at her. 'Are you OK?'

'I'm fine,' she says, giving me a hug. She struggles to sit up. 'Come on! We're going! Pass me my coat.'

'But . . . the doctor says he's admitting you!'

'Over my dead body! Where are my shoes?'

'Here.' I line them up for her and help her off the bed as she manoeuvres her feet into them.

She seems awkward and I wonder if her dead leg is still playing her up. She pulls her coat on and looks around for her bag.

Then the curtain is pulled back and the doctor walks in, studying his notes. 'Good news. I've managed to find you a bed –' he says, then he looks up. 'What's going on?'

'I'm going home,' says Mum, standing very straight.

'I don't think that's a good idea, Mrs Campbell. You've had a nasty fall.'

'Nothing's broken, you said so yourself,' she says reasonably.

I breathe a sigh of relief. But the doctor's not listening.

'That's not the point. I've already explained to you, I think it's important that we get to the bottom of why you keep having these bumps and falls. I'd like to do some tests . . .'

'I'm afraid that's not possible,' says Mum in her haughtiest voice. 'I'm discharging myself, as I believe I am perfectly entitled to do.' She doesn't sound like my mum. She sounds like Mrs Shepherd putting a naughty pupil in their place. I feel really proud of her. She's more than a match for the young doctor.

'I can't stop you if you are determined to leave,' he says, looking cross. 'But I strongly advise you to visit your GP. I am concerned that your tiredness, your clumsiness, your general condition may be an indicator of something more serious. I would like to –'

'Thank you for your concern, Doctor,' says Mum, interrupting him in mid-flow, which surprises me because she's never normally rude. 'I will visit my GP, I assure you. Now, give me whatever I need to sign to get me out of this place. Come on, Tasheika.'

She puts her bag on her shoulder and sweeps past him. By the time Miss Webb has managed to find a parking space and has turned up at A & E we are ready to go.

Chapter 15

'Is everything OK?'

'What did Mrs Shepherd want you for?'

'We were so worried!'

'You're not in trouble, are you?'

'We thought you'd been suspended.' This last from Chantelle, one of the Barbies.

I've hardly set foot in school before I'm surrounded by a gaggle of girls all demanding to know why I'd been dragged out of class by the headmistress the previous day.

'It was my mum. She collapsed at work but she's OK now.'

'Oh, that's good,' says Chantelle, sounding disappointed. 'Nothing serious then?'

'No, nothing serious.'

'Leave her alone!' says Lissa and for once I'm glad of her bossiness because everyone shuts up.

She and Dani and Ali had all rung me last night and I'd explained to them my mum had fallen but there was no harm done, she was back home again. But the Barbies love to make a drama out of a crisis.

'What happened then?' persists Zadie.

I can feel everyone staring at me. But I can also see Mum's worried face and hear her voice, warning me and the boys this morning before she left for work: 'Don't say anything at school about me falling yesterday. Remember – people don't need to know our business.'

Then, thankfully, Miss Webb says, 'Quiet, everyone. I want to take the register,' and everybody takes their seat.

My form teacher was really good last night. She insisted on dropping Mum and me home from the hospital when Mum told her she'd been discharged. (It was only a white lie.)

'No thank you, we'll be fine. I've got to collect my son from nursery first,' Mum had said.

'We can pick him up in the car. It's quicker than walking.'

Mum hesitated and checked her watch. We were late already. 'I don't want to impose any further on your kindness,' she said reluctantly.

'Honestly, it's no problem,' said Miss Webb. Then she laughed. 'You'd be doing me a favour actually. I'll be in trouble with the head if she knows I let you find your own way home.'

I looked at her in surprise. I never knew the teachers were afraid of the head too. But Mum laughed too like it was a joke and got into the front seat next to her. And then they chatted all the way to the nursery, mostly about me and how well I was doing at school, which was nice but a bit embarrassing.

Afterwards, Miss Webb drove us home and the two of them carried on chatting like bezzies in the front while a very excited Keneil bounced up and down in his seat-belt next to me in the back. I was kind of listening to them talking about the schools they'd gone to and then I realized with a shock from what they were saying that they must be more or less the same age. Which was weird because I think of my form teacher as really young but I don't think of Mum as that young because she's my mum and she's got four kids.

As we got closer to home, Mum went quiet. 'You can drop us off here,' she said even though we were still on the main road.

But Miss Webb turned into the estate. 'No, honestly, it's no trouble. Which one is it?'

Mum pointed to our block and my teacher pulled up in front of it. One of the bins had been upended, spilling its contents out on the road. Some boys were chucking the rubbish at each other and when Mum got out of the car she told them to pick it up. They swore at her and ran off and she was ashamed in front of my teacher, you could tell.

I was too.

But Miss Webb didn't seem bothered in the least. 'Which floor are you on?'

'The tenth,' answered Mum, helping Keneil out of the back.

'Let me give you a hand up with your bags.'

'That won't be necessary,' said Mum abruptly and Miss Webb stared at her in surprise. She sounded so formal, you see, but she'd been friendly up to now, chatting away to my teacher in the car like they were mates. Then she took her purse out of her bag and said, 'How much do I owe you?' like Miss Webb was a taxi.

After that it got really awkward with Mum pushing money into my teacher's hand and my teacher saying 'No!' and pushing it back at her. In the end Mum grabbed Keneil and said, 'Thank

86

you very much,' in a snooty voice and then she turned away, leaving my teacher with a ten-pound note in her hand.

'Tasheika,' said Miss Webb looking upset, 'I can't accept this. Please give it back to your mum when you get a chance.'

'Yes, Miss,' I said miserably, tucking it in my pocket and wondering how it had all gone wrong. I don't know whether you're supposed to offer to pay someone who gives you a lift but I just knew Mum had handled it badly. She'd come over rude, like she was with the doctor. But this time I don't think she'd meant to be.

I knew why she'd done it. She was embarrassed by the rubbish and the boys swearing. She didn't want my teacher to think we were all like that round here. She wanted to prove we were better than that.

Miss Webb gazed up silently at our tower block. I wondered if she was thinking she was glad she didn't live here. But then she said, 'Tenth floor! That's a long way up. You must have an amazing view from up there.' And she sounded like she really meant it.

'Yes, Miss,' I repeated. And I wanted to say, *Come up and see for yourself*, because she was right, it was amazing. But I knew Mum wouldn't like it so I didn't.

This morning in English the whole class is working peacefully, heads bent over their books. I look up, enjoying the silence. Next to me Ali is concentrating hard, the tip of her tongue just visible between her teeth as she writes down her answers. Miss Webb is sitting at her desk, marking. She catches my eye and smiles at me then returns to her pile of books.

I thought I'd miss the buzz of my primary school when I came to Riverside but the truth is I love it here. And nobody would believe me – crazy, fun-loving Tash – but it's not just because of the fashion show and netball and my lovely friends in the No Secrets Club.

What I really love is an ordinary lesson like this. A slightly boring lesson with no surprises.

It's peaceful and predictable, you see. The opposite of home.

I never know what to expect there any more.

Chapter 16

On Saturday I pull back my bedroom curtains and groan. Outside, the rain is lashing down. Mum needs to rest up but it's hard because we're all stuck inside. I try to keep my brothers quiet but they've got loads of energy to get rid of after a week at school and they end up squabbling and punching each other. What is it with boys? Like, do girls thump each other when they're bored? I keep warning them to keep the noise down because Mum's trying to have a lie-in but they forget.

I wish I could take them out somewhere. A football match, maybe? They'd love that, sitting in the stand, supporting West Park Wanderers! Maybe Alana de Silva would be there too, cheering on her boyfriend, Titch Mooney? But we can't afford it. We don't have a tin marked FOOTBALL.

Eventually, Mum gets up. 'Thanks, Tash, for keeping an eye on them; you're a good girl,' she says. But she still looks tired and her words sound slurred as if she's still half-asleep. She flops down on the sofa and stares blankly at the telly with the boys. At least they calm down with her sitting between them.

I make cheese on toast for us all and try to clean up a bit and then, late afternoon, when the rain stops at last, we all go out shopping, Mum included.

We go to the outdoor market to buy food. I like it here best first thing in the morning when it's full of bustle and the different stalls are piled high with vegetables, meat, fish, flowers, cheeses, breads, cakes – you name it, it's there. The sight and smell of them all could drive you mad. But now it's late and the crowds have gone and they're starting to sell off their produce, which is better for us because we get bargains.

They all know us in the market. The butcher teases Keneil and Devon who are staring round-eyed at the dead hare hanging off his stall, fur still intact, and he slips in some extra sausages for us. Mad Maggie, who's as old as the hills and spends her life shuffling round the market, pats

Keneil on the head even though she swears at most people. When Mum buys her bread the lady gives us a bag of broken biscuits to take home as well. We buy potatoes and carrots and swede and onions for a stew at our veg stall, plus loads of squashy, knocked-down tomatoes for spaghetti Bolognese and a massive bag of apples for practically nothing.

'They're all bruised,' I point out.

'That's all right, I'll make apple crumble for tea,' Mum says. She seems to have perked up a bit now she's out in the fresh air.

'Apple crumble and cream?' asks Marlon longingly.

She checks her purse. 'OK,' she agrees, 'for a treat.' She buys a carton of clotted cream *and* a jar of gooseberry jam as well, and Marlon's face lights up like a beacon. I'm *so* glad Miss Webb won the battle of the ten-pound note.

We're done at the market and about to go home when Marlon suddenly remembers something. 'Mum, I need a new PE shirt for Monday. I've lost mine.'

Mum's face clouds over. 'Why didn't you tell me before?'

'I *did*!' he says and it's true, I heard him.

'Did you?' She looks confused.

Marlon's face creases up in panic. 'I've got to have one for Monday, Mum, or Mr Wilton will go crazy . . .'

'OK, OK,' says Mum, calming him down. Marlon hates getting into trouble. 'We'll pop along to the shopping centre, they sell them at Barrington's.' She looks down at our heavy bags full of vegetables and food shopping and sighs. 'Everyone, grab one.'

It takes longer than we thought to get to the centre. Keneil wants to help but his bag is too heavy for him. Devon drags his along the pavement and makes a hole in it and then the handles on mine break and stuff rolls out on to the pavement. In the end we pile everything into the two biggest, strongest bags and Mum and I take one each and haul them up the road. By the time we get inside, Mum is worn out again.

'Look,' I say to Mum, 'you stay here with Keneil. Marlon, come with me and we'll get the shirt.'

Mum takes up my offer gratefully and sinks down on to a bench. Devon starts to trail after me and I say sharply, 'Go back to Mum! You don't have to follow me everywhere!' He turns straight back without a word and I feel harsh. But that bag was really heavy and, to tell the truth, I've had enough of looking after my little brothers today.

I glance back at Mum. She's closed her eyes and looks like she's having a kip. Honest, sometimes *I* feel like the mum around here, not her!

We find the shirt and are queuing up at the till when I hear, 'Tash! Tash!'

Oh no! I turn round and all my fears are realized. The Barbies, all three of them, are grinning at us like Cheshire cats.

Georgia: 'Just seen Ali and Lissa. They've been hanging out together.'

Oh. Great.

Chantelle: 'Aren't you going to introduce us then?'

'This is my brother, Marlon.'

'Hi, Marlon!' they chorus. Shy at the best of times, my brother, confronted by all this unsolicited female attention, casts his eyes to the floor and is promptly struck dumb.

Zadie: 'Awwh! He's shy.'

Chantelle: 'OMG! He's so cute!'

'Can he speak? Or is there . . . you know . . .

something wrong with him?' This last from Georgia in a stage whisper.

'Georgia!' The other two start squealing at her as Georgia protests loudly, 'I'm not being mean! I was just wondering!' and Marlon raises his eyes to mine in desperation.

'Got to go,' I say firmly, grabbing him by the elbow. 'My mum's waiting for us.'

'Your *mum's* here! Where is she?' Georgia's eyes light up and my heart sinks. She is sooo nosy. 'Come on, everyone. Let's go and say hello to Tash's mum.'

'Sorry! We're in a bit of a rush!' I say, turning away.

Georgia: 'It won't take a minute.'

Chantelle: 'I can't wait to meet her. I feel like I know her already from your talk in English.'

Zadie: 'What about your other brothers? Are they here too?'

I sigh, deeply regretting that talk on the second day of term entitled *All About Me*. I'd gone overboard, wanting to impress Miss Webb with my very first homework. Wanting to impress everyone, if I'm honest. I'd gone on and on about my family: what a great mum I had; how she looked after us all so well; how she was good at everything – cooking, knitting, sewing; how cute my little brothers were . . .

Well, she *is* a great mum, so there, and they *are* cute! I take a deep breath and sail back to where I'd beached her and the boys, with the Barbies behind me squawking like demented ducklings and Marlon morosely bringing up the rear.

When I get to the bench Mum is slumped over, fast asleep. What is she doing? Only down-and-outs sleep in the centre. There's no sign of Devon or Keneil.

'Mum?' I touch her shoulder, gently at first and then give her a shake. 'Mum? Wake up! Where are the boys?'

She opens her eyes and looks at me blankly. A thin dribble of spittle is trickling down her chin. Behind me Chantelle whispers, 'Is that her mum?'

'Tasheika?' says Mum, struggling to sit up straight. It's as if she doesn't really recognize me.

'Good afternoon, Mrs Campbell,' says Georgia, stepping forward and putting her hand out. 'Pleased to meet you. I'm Georgia, a friend of Tash's.'

Mum stares at her and takes her hand limply. 'I'm Zadie.'

'I'm Chantelle.'

'Pleasedtomeetyou,' echoes Mum, the words running into each other.

'Where are the boys?' I repeat and she looks confused and struggles to her feet. But her bad leg gives way beneath her and she falls back on to the bench.

'Is she drunk?' I hear Georgia whisper and I want to die.

'NO!' snaps Marlon so fiercely Georgia recoils. Immediately I feel proud of my normally gentle kid brother for sticking up for my mum and ashamed of myself for not doing so.

'I don't know. They were here . . . Where've they gone? . . . Only a minute ago . . . Keneil?' She looks around vaguely, her words jumbled, like she can't work out what's going on. The Barbies exchange a look.

Then, just as I think things can't get any worse, Marlon says, 'There they are!'

They're coming out of the big new sweetshop that opened last week. Escorted by a burly security guard.

Chapter 17

It doesn't take long for word to get around.

'What are *they* up to?' says Dani disdainfully, looking across at the Barbies at Monday breaktime. My stomach lurches. I knew there was something up when I came in this morning and was greeted by a chorus of 'Hi, Tash!' from the evil trio, who then immediately broke rank and sat down in their seats, the picture of innocence.

Now they're in a huddle in the corner of the playground like witches round a cauldron, alternately whispering, laughing raucously and then hushing each other and managing, thereby, to attract loads of attention. Before long they are surrounded by girls, dying to find out what's going on. Which is obviously their intention.

'No good, I bet,' says Ali gloomily. 'They are *so* annoying!'

I shift uncomfortably on the bench. People are glancing over in our direction.

'They're talking about *us*!' says Lissa in surprise. She springs to her feet. 'I'm going to find out what's going on!'

'No, don't!' I protest, but Dani says, 'I'm coming with you!' and they head off to confront the Barbies.

Ali, less brave than the rest of us, looks at me as I remain seated. 'Aren't you going too?'

I shake my head and, surprised, she asks, 'Why not?'

'I already know what's going on.'

'What?'

I groan and bury my head in my hands. 'Believe me, whatever they're saying, it's not true.'

By the end of breaktime everyone in my form knows.

I *hate* the Barbies.

'It wasn't my fault!' Devon had insisted all the way home.

'Are you in charge of these two?' the security guard had asked Mum and immediately I thought, *Oh no, what have they done?* Behind me I could hear the Barbies giving little gasps of delight. Even if

Mum wanted to deny it (I did!) she couldn't, because as soon as Keneil spotted her he yelled, 'Mum!' and dashed straight into her arms.

'Where did you get to, you naughty boys?' she said. Keneil was looking his normal happy self but Devon was scared, you could tell. 'You know you're not supposed to wander off!'

'Could you step inside the shop, madam? We'd like a word.' His voice was polite but cold. An order rather than a question.

Mum's lips tightened and she frowned at Devon.

'What have you done now?' she said crossly and a tear rolled down his cheek.

'It wasn't me, it was Keneil.'

We all stared at my littlest brother who took in our serious faces, opened his mouth and howled. Loudly. So loudly the whole shopping centre stopped and stared too. At least, that's what it felt like.

'Come this way please, madam,' said the security guard and without another word Mum grabbed Keneil and Devon firmly by the hand, one on each side, and strode into the sweetshop, her head held high.

Marlon and I both picked up a heavy bag and

followed them. Behind me I could hear Chantelle's excited voice.

'OMG! They're being arrested! The whole family!'

Now Tasheika Campbell and her errant family are trending on the Barbie grapevine.

I manage to get through the next lesson by devising enterprising ways of seeing off Georgia, Chantelle and Zadie forever and sketching them out in my rough book. Witches should be burned at the stake but the guillotine seems the most satisfactory method, maybe because we're in French. Madame Dupré tells me off for not paying attention so I make the blade even bigger and sharper and add her decapitated head to the others in the basket. Beside me, Ali giggles nervously.

At lunchtime I lead the way to the picnic tables, with the rest of the No Secrets Club in tow. The Barbies are already there. Dani, Lissa and I glare at them and they get up and move away.

'Thank you,' calls Ali politely after them. We glare at her too. 'Sorry,' she says guiltily as we take their seats. 'Force of habit.'

'Right then. Tell us all!' says Lissa, taking charge as usual.

'What are they saying?'

'That you and your family were all arrested for shoplifting on Saturday.'

I groan. 'No, we weren't! Nobody was arrested.'

'Did you get away with it?' asks Dani with interest.

'No! Nobody was shoplifting! My little brother Keneil helped himself to some pick 'n' mix from the new sweetshop in the centre, that's all.'

'Oh, I love it there!' she says. 'Have you tried their sherbert lemons?'

'Shut up, Dani!' says Lissa. 'Let Tash explain.'

'That's it. He's only three. He just saw this big stack of sweets and he ate a few. He didn't even know he was doing wrong.'

'Shops do that on purpose,' says Ali, who knows all about consumerism and stuff like that. 'You can't blame the kids. They put sweets on display to tempt them. They do it in supermarkets too. They deliberately put chocolate in their line of sight near the checkouts.'

'I know, my sister used to have a right paddy in Tesco. It was really embarrassing,' says Dani with feeling.

'What happened?' Lissa asks me, ignoring the others.

'He was in the shop with Devon so the security guard came out and told my mum and Mum went in and paid for them. It only came to twenty-four pence.'

'Is that it?' says Ali. 'Big deal! The Barbies need to get a life. What a fuss about nothing.'

Dani and Lissa look at each other and all goes ominously quiet.

'What?' I ask flatly. 'What else have they been saying?'

'Nothing!' says Lissa.

'Time for netball practice!' says Dani, jumping up.

'Tell me!' I say. 'No secrets, remember?'

'Okaayy,' says Lissa, licking her lips nervously. 'It's really stupid –'

'And no one believes it –' adds Dani.

'It's just the Barbies –'

'You know what they're like –'

'TELL ME!' I shout, and they both exchange glances again.

Then Lissa takes a deep breath. 'Actually,' she says, 'they're saying your mum was drunk.'

Chapter 18

'WHAT?'

Two tell-tale patches of pink flare up in Lissa's cheeks.

'Of course she wasn't drunk!' I snap. 'Don't be stupid!'

'Don't shoot the messenger,' she snaps back. 'You did ask.'

'My mum doesn't even drink!' I say wildly and Ali says, 'We know that,' which is a lie because none of them have even met my mum. She could be a total, off-her-head, falling-down drunk for all they know.

'She was just repeating what they were saying,' explains Dani.

'What everyone is saying,' mutters Lissa, cross that I'd called her stupid. But then she sees my face and adds quickly, 'We didn't believe them,

Tash, honest we didn't!' and I know she means it.

'No,' I say, upset to the core. 'But everyone else will!'

We had to go to netball then. I was rubbish. I couldn't concentrate. I was aware of people watching me off court, people talking about me, sniggering. I wanted to stop playing and yell at them all. Instead, I kept missing the ball. In the end Mrs Waters got cross and told me off in front of everyone.

'Keep your mind on the game, Tasheika! You're in a world of your own!'

It made people talk even more.

Afterwards she calls me over. 'Is anything the matter?' she asks.

'No, Miss!' I say, because from the corner of my eye I can see the Barbies earwigging.

She eyes me doubtfully. 'Then pull yourself together. We've got the first match this week and if you play like that we've got no chance.'

'No, Miss.'

'I have high hopes for you, Tash. Don't let me down.'

'No, Miss.'

'And don't let the team down either. You're captain, remember?'

'No, Miss. I mean, yes, Miss.'

All afternoon I sit in class worrying: worrying about letting Mrs Waters down; worrying about letting the team down; worrying about letting Mum down. Worrying about what Chantelle was whispering to Tori, and Georgia was whispering to Ella. Worrying about what was in the note that Zadie passed to Emma, which Emma passed to Chloe, which Chloe passed to Nisha.

I get told off again.

At the end of the day I don't feel like yelling at anyone any more. I just want to go home.

'See you, Tash!' calls Ali as I grab my stuff and dash off.

I wave without looking back and shout, 'See you!'

I don't even feel like talking to my best friend.

When Mum came home from work I didn't want to talk to her either.

It was all her fault.

All through tea I sit in silence. It was nice. Stew. She'd made it earlier that day, between jobs, from the vegetables we'd bought at the market. I couldn't eat it though.

'What's wrong?' she asks afterwards when the boys have cleared away and are sitting watching telly.

'Nothing.'

'Yes, there is.' She comes over to the sink where I'm squirting water into the washing-up bowl and puts her arms round me. 'What is it, babe?'

I shrug her off. 'Nothing. Don't keep on.'

She switches on a CD and picks up a tea towel. Reggae belts out as she begins to wipe the soapy dishes I'm stacking on the draining board and she sways in time to the music, humming quietly to herself. Standing next to her, I refuse to join in like I normally would, so she bumps me with her hip, trying to get me moving.

'Grow up!' I say.

'I am grown-up, Grumpy Guts!' she says with a cheeky grin. 'I'll be thirty-three on Friday!'

She doesn't look it, dancing next to me in her jeans and vest top. I don't respond. Instead, I hand her a saucepan, too big to join the dishes on the draining board, and as I do I notice a big plaster on her finger.

'What's that?'

She glances down. 'My fault. I nearly added

my finger to the stew when I was chopping the veg.'

'You should be more careful.' My tone is surly, more impatient than concerned, and she glances at me in surprise.

'Yes, you're right, I should.' She picks up another bowl but it slips from her hand and falls with a clatter into the washing-up bowl. Soap suds splash up over my school uniform and I jump backwards.

'Mu-um! What are you doing? You clumsy idiot! Just go away!'

I expect her to laugh and flick more suds at me but, instead, she drops the tea towel and grips the edge of the worktop, her head bent. I stare at her, suddenly frightened. *Say something, Mum.*

At last, she says in a quiet little voice, 'I'll leave you to it then,' and turns to Keneil, who has wandered in, and gives him a hug. 'Mummy's going to work,' she says. 'See you later. Be a good boy for your sister.' She straightens up and adds, 'I'm sorry, Tash,' and my heart lurches as I see that her eyes are full of tears. Then she puts on her coat and she's gone, without even putting my little brother to bed.

I pick up the tea towel off the floor where she

dropped it and finish the washing up. I see to Keneil: milk, teeth, story, kiss, cuddle, light out. I listen to Devon read, remind the boys to clean their teeth, chivvy them into bed, ignore their protests.

I need to be on my own. To think.

I curl up in the armchair, tight as a spring in the now-silent flat, waiting for my mum to come home. Ali phones but I ignore her. I've got science homework to do but I ignore that too. Instead, I stare at the blank television screen and chew the skin round my nails till it's raw.

I hate her. I hate my mum. She expects too much from me.

She's stupid. She's so clumsy. She's always falling over and bumping into things and chopping her fingers off. No wonder people think she's an alcoholic. She's *embarrassing*!

A thought occurs to me. Maybe they're right! Maybe she is an alkie after all! Maybe she's got a secret stash of booze?

I jump up and run around the flat, pulling open kitchen cupboards, slamming them shut. I search under the sink, in her wardrobe, in drawers, the bathroom cabinet, I even rummage through the airing cupboard. But there's nothing.

Zilch. Not even a single leftover bottle of sherry from Christmas.

So? Maybe she does her drinking elsewhere? What if she hasn't got three jobs after all? What if she goes out socializing instead?

But I know – I know – none of this is true. That's not my mum. She never drinks, she thinks it's a waste of money and she's seen the effect it has on some people living round here. I remember her face when she left the flat. She was crying. Tears start spilling down my cheeks too.

She loves us. I know she does.

But maybe she's sick and tired of looking after us all on her own, 24/7? Maybe she's had enough and she just can't do it any more? Like Dad.

Dad loved us too, Mum said. But he had enough and he went away.

I'm scared rigid.

The door opens and Mum walks in. I burst into tears.

'Tash?' she says. 'Sweetheart? Whatever's the matter?' She comes over and folds me into her arms.

'Mum!' I wail. 'What's going on?'

Chapter 19

I don't tell her what everyone else is saying about her. Instead, I hear myself moaning in big, shuddering sobs, 'Don't you love us any more?'

'What?' She pulls away from me, holding me at arm's-length and looks me straight in the eyes. 'Of course I love you, silly. I love you kids more than anything, you know that. You're the whole world to me.' I know she's telling the truth.

'You're not going to leave us, are you?'

'I'd never leave you, you know that.'

'Dad did.'

She rolls her eyes. 'Is that what all this is about? I'm not your dad. Anyway, he didn't leave you, he left me. Ages ago. I'm still here, aren't I? You've got me for good whether you like it or not. Come here, dafty.'

She sinks down on to the sofa and gives me

a hug. I put my arms round her and squeeze her tight, pressing my face into her neck. She smells nice, even though she's been cleaning all day. She always smells nice. Her breath tickles my ear.

'What brought all this on?'

'I'm worried about you.'

'Why?'

'Nothing.'

'Tell me. I won't be cross, I promise.'

I stare up at her, into her brown eyes just like mine.

'You've changed, Mum. I don't like it.'

I expect her to be offended but instead she looks sad, so sad that my tears start flowing again. But I keep going, trying to explain between sobs. 'You're tired all the time. And you keep bumping into things . . . and falling down . . . and dropping stuff . . .'

It's coming out all wrong. Suddenly I let out a big long wail. 'I'm scaaaaared!' And even though I'm criticizing her, her arms tighten round me. I snuggle down into them and stop crying as she shushes and rocks me like a baby. I'm eleven years old and nearly as big as her but it still feels nice. I'm loving the closeness, loving having her all to myself for once. It's OK, Mum's here, Mum's making it all right again. She always does.

Then she says something that totally freaks me out.

'I know,' she says in a low voice. 'I am too.'

I sit bolt upright. That's not what I wanted to hear. 'Why? Do you think there's something wrong with you?'

Immediately she laughs, turning it into a joke. 'Yeah, loads! But nothing that a boob job and some Botox wouldn't put right.'

Despite myself, I laugh too. It's so not true. My mum's beautiful.

'My friend Ali thinks all that stuff is really bad.'

'Your friend Ali is right. She's the one who's Alana de Silva's sister, yeah?'

'Yeah.'

'She sounds nice. And your other two friends. What are they called, remind me?'

'Lissa and Dani.'

'That's it, Lissa and Dani. The Gang of Four, I remember.'

'The No Secrets Club.'

'What?'

'That's what we call ourselves now. The No

Secrets Club. We promised we'd tell each other everything.'

Mum's eyes open wide in alarm and I add quickly, 'Don't worry. I haven't said a word about you going out to work at night. Or being in hospital. I won't.'

She looks relieved. 'Good girl, Tash.' She strokes my hair back behind my ear and says thoughtfully, 'You'll have to invite them round one day so I can meet them all. Would you like that?'

I nod furiously. They can see for themselves then that my mum is no alkie. 'When you're feeling better.'

'I'm feeling better already,' she says, then adds impulsively, 'Blow it! Tell them to come to tea on Friday. It's my birthday and I'm going to take the day off!'

'Are you sure?' I ask uncertainly.

'Yes. Absolutely. We'll have party tea. I could do with some fun and the boys will love it. We'll have balloons and streamers and play Pass the Parcel!'

'We're too old for that!'

'You're never too old for Pass the Parcel! Anyway, it's *my* birthday, I decide!'

We grin at each other. I love it when Mum is silly.

'OK, I'll ask them. I don't know if they'll come though. Maybe we should just ask Ali?'

'No, I want to meet them all. You've told me so much about them I want to meet them in the flesh. Ali's the serious one, Dani's the tomboy and Lissa's the posh one, is that right?'

'Sort of.'

'Good. I can't wait. Now then, let's watch telly for a bit before we go to bed. Done your homework?'

'Yes,' I lie, because I want to stay here with her. We snuggle down happily together on the sofa and she presses the remote control.

'Mum?'

'Yes?'

'Will you go to the GP?'

'What for?'

'To find out what's wrong with you.'

'I'm fine!'

'No you're not, you keep dropping things and stuff.'

'I'm just clumsy!'

'The doctor in the hospital said you should.'

'He was an old fusspot . . .'

'No he wasn't, he was young. Pleeeease, Mum! For me?'

She sighs heavily. 'Yes, all right then. Just to stop you going on. There's nothing wrong with me a good night's sleep won't cure.'

'When?'

'Sometime soon.'

'This week?'

'If I can get an appointment.'

'Promise?'

'Promise. Now shut up, I'm watching.'

I smile to myself. Everything is going to be all right after all. Mum's back to normal.

I can't wait to show her off to my friends.

Chapter 20

Ali is so excited she is coming to tea. To my surprise Lissa and Dani say they can come too. Dani's as bad as me, she never meets up with the others at weekends, and I wasn't sure if Lissa would even want to after her remarks about the hooligans on our estate. She does though.

'It's my mum's birthday,' I explain at breaktime at our favourite picnic table. 'I warn you, she's doing party tea. It's for my little brothers really,' I add hastily.

'I love party tea!' squeals Lissa. 'I haven't had it for ages!'

'It gets worse. We're going to play party games as well. Pass the Parcel, Pin the Tail on the Donkey, Dead Lions . . .'

'What about Simon Says?' Dani grins. 'That's my favourite.'

'Or Statues! I always win Statues!' shrieks Lissa.

'We can do some dancing if you like,' I suggest. 'My mum's a brilliant dancer.'

'Your mum sounds cool,' says Lissa and I feel a warm glow inside.

'Devon is too. He's into break-dancing. He could show you how to do it if you want.'

'Yeeaaah!' cheers Ali, but Dani says, 'Can't we play football?' and we all groan. Dani is totally obsessed with football.

'You can go out to play with Marlon,' I suggest. 'He'd rather play footie than dance any day.'

'OK!' says Dani, brightening up. 'You're on!'

'Will Ajay be there?' asks Lissa innocently.

'Ajay? Why would he be at my mum's birthday?'

'No, I mean, will he be . . . you know . . . around?'

'How would I know?' I say, then Dani chants, 'Lis-sa – for – Ajay! Lis-sa – for – Ajay!' and we all laugh as her cheeks turn pink.

'I just wondered, that's all,' she says, making out she doesn't care, but she doesn't fool anyone. Lissa's got the hots for Ajay. No wonder she wants to come to my place.

I wonder what her mum would think about that? I met her mum at the fashion show and she's really posh. I've seen how she fusses round

Lissa when she picks her up from netball too. Something tells me she wouldn't like it one little bit.

Today, for the first time since I started at Riverside Academy for Girls, I wasn't looking forward to coming to school. I thought the Barbies would still be milking the story about my mum being a drunk for all it was worth. But people seem to have lost interest in it, probably because they can hear us chatting about coming to mine for tea on Friday. I mean, *obviously* I wouldn't have invited them if my mum was a dipsomaniac, would I? A dipsomaniac is someone with a chronic alcohol problem, by the way.

Anyway, some of us have got other things on our minds. Like our first netball match for instance.

We practise netball skills at lunchtime. I'm really good today, though I say so myself. Mrs Waters must have thought so too because she says at the end, 'Well done, Tash. Much, much better. Play like that on Thursday and we'll thrash the opposition.'

I float into double science on a cloud of happiness. Midway through the lesson the teacher tells Dani to collect the homework and my heart misses a beat. I'd meant to get up early and do it but it had gone completely out of my head. *Say nothing and Miss Riddle won't notice.* I give a tiny shake of my head when Dani comes to me and luckily she moves on without a fuss. I've got away with it.

Or so I thought. At the end of the afternoon, I come crashing down to earth.

'Stay behind, Tasheika Campbell,' says Miss Riddle when the bell goes and Dani looks at me in alarm. *Uh-oh!* I stand meekly in front of my science teacher until everyone's left the room, then she hands me a detention slip.

'What's this for?' I say, still hoping I can wing it.

She raises one eyebrow. 'Did you think I wouldn't notice you hadn't handed in your homework?'

I must have been mad. Miss Riddle has eyes in the back of her head. There's no point in making an excuse. I stare glumly at the slip of paper in my hand and then I gulp.

The detention is for Thursday, after school. The night of the netball match.

'I can't do this, Miss.'

'I BEG YOUR PARDON?' Miss Riddle, tall, thin and severe-looking, glares down at me through the glasses perched on the end of her long nose and I feel myself wilting. She's always been nice to me till now because normally I'm good at science. But I've seen other people fall foul of her.

Why oh why didn't I do my homework?

Because last night I was worried sick about Mum, that's why. And, afterwards, when it was all sorted, I was enjoying snuggling up with her and then, this morning, I clean forgot!

'I'll get into trouble . . .'

'You are already in trouble. That's why you have a detention.'

'But I'll be in even more trouble . . .'

'You should have thought about that before you failed to do your homework.'

'But, Miss! Can I do it another day instead?'

'Absolutely not! That detention is arranged for my convenience, not yours! Now I want that detention slip signed by your parents and returned to me.'

'Yes, Miss,' I say miserably and exit quickly before she decides to give me another one for arguing.

Outside the others are waiting for me.

'How did you get on?' asks Ali anxiously. I'm about to show her the detention slip when I notice the Barbies hovering like mosquitoes, waiting to take a bite at me.

'Did you get a detention?' asks Georgia eagerly and I say, 'No, of course not!' in my best scornful tone and slip it into my pocket instead, away from prying eyes. 'I've got to do my homework tonight.'

'Ohhh!' says Georgia, sounding disappointed, and the three blood-suckers fade away in search of juicier prey.

And then, to make things even more complicated, Mrs Waters goes past and holds up her thumbs to us. 'All set for Thursday, girls?' she says, sounding as excited as we are about the match.

'Yes, Miss!' shout Lissa and Dani.

She looks at me. 'Ready, Captain?'

'Ready, Miss.' There is NO WAY I can let her down.

So here's the problem: how on earth can I be in two places at once?

Chapter 21

Forget that problem. I've got an even worse one now.

How can I be in *three* places at once?!

Thursday morning and I still haven't solved the first one. I don't know how to. I've been awake all night, tossing and turning, trying to work out what to do after school.

I want to play in the netball match, obviously. I'm the captain! If I don't, I'll let everyone down.

But if I don't do Miss Riddle's detention, it's more than my life's worth. Hardly anyone gets a detention at Riverside and NOBODY misses one. I could be expelled!

Then, just when I think things couldn't get any worse, Mum says, 'Oh, I nearly forgot, Tash. I've made that appointment at the doctor's.'

'Oh good. When is it?'

'This afternoon.'

My blood runs cold. 'What time?'

'Four thirty. I know you don't normally collect Keneil from the nursery on a Thursday but do you mind doing it today for once? I shouldn't be long.'

'But, Mum! I've got a netball match! I *told* you!'

'Damn! So you did! I completely forgot. I made it for today because it's my afternoon off.' She groans. 'Now what shall I do?'

'Make it earlier! In school time.'

'They're not open then.'

I stare at her blankly.

'Oh, I'll manage!' she mutters crossly. 'I'll take him with me. What time will you be home?'

'I'm not sure.'

'Right. I'll have to take the others with me as well,' she says, looking really fed up.

'Why?'

'Well, I can't leave them alone in the flat if you don't know how long you're going to be. Oh, maybe I'll just cancel the appointment!'

'No, don't do that!'

It had been hard enough getting her to make it and deep down I knew she needed to sort out what was wrong. I think hard. No matter if I play netball or go to my detention, I should be more or less finished by four thirty. 'Tell you what, Mum, after the match I'll rush along to the doctor's as fast as I can. With a bit of luck you won't have gone in by then.'

'Are you sure? They're always running late at the surgery. You can look after the boys in the waiting room for me.'

'Sorted.'

'You're a good girl, Tash,' she says and gives me a kiss as she goes out of the door. 'What would I do without you?'

Me, a good girl? Tell that to Miss Riddle!

No, there's no need for Mum to find out I've got a detention. She'd go ballistic!

Instead, Marlon signs my detention slip for me. He's got really neat writing for a ten-year-old.

I still have a choice to make.

Netball/detention? Detention/netball?

It's like playing a real-life game of Would You Rather?

Question: Would you rather let your friends down or get into serious trouble at school?

Answer: I'd rather not let down my friends, obviously.

But if I get into trouble at school, I'm letting my mum down. And myself.

What am I going to do? I don't know! It's too hard! By last lesson on Thursday afternoon I still haven't made up my mind.

'What's wrong?' whispers Ali who can read me like a book.

'Tell you later,' I whisper back as Grumpy Griffiths frowns at us. I give up. I can't make this decision on my own. I need my friends to help me decide what to do. And, knowing that, a strange, warm feeling of relief sweeps through my body.

But then, the door opens and Miss Riddle puts her head round and says, 'Excuse me, Mr Griffiths. Would you mind if I had a word with Tasheika Campbell?' and my blood freezes again. I get up and walk out of the classroom with everyone's eyes on me. She's come to escort me to my detention; now everyone will know.

Outside the door she says, 'Detention slip, please.' I hand it to her and she reads it. 'Marlon Campbell?'

'My father, Miss.'

She nods, then to my surprise tears the slip in two.

'I'm afraid something has come up, Tasheika. I have an urgent, unavoidable appointment and am unable to supervise your detention after school. Therefore, as it is my fault, I will excuse you from the arrangement.'

'Miss?'

'It means you don't have to do your detention. Just this once. But, Tasheika Campbell, one more stunt like that and you will be in serious trouble.'

'Yes, Miss. Absolutely! Sorry, Miss.'

'And apologize to your father for me for the change of plan.'

'My father?' For a second I wonder what she's going on about then my brain kicks into gear. 'Of course! No problem. Thank you, Miss Riddle!'

The bell goes and people start pouring out of the classroom. Ali appears at my elbow, and hands me my bag. 'What did she want?' she asks anxiously.

'Nothing important,' I call back happily over my shoulder as Dani and Lissa grab me by the arms and whisk me away.

'Come on, Captain!' says Lissa. 'No time to chat! The other team will be here in a minute and we need you!'

Chapter 22

Lissa was wrong for once. They weren't here in a minute. They weren't here for ages. We were running really late and I could feel myself hopping from one foot to the other, starting to fret. Lots of mums, Lissa's and Ali's included, turn up to watch (not mine of course) but there's no sign of the bus. Then at last it appears and a cheer goes up.

They pour off the bus, large, loud and confident, looking like they're going to walk all over us. But, to my surprise, as soon as we make a start, I realize they're not that good after all. Not as good as us, anyway. It must be all the practice we've been doing.

We've worked out a strategy, you see, and that's what wins the game for us. That and our superior skill, of course! Depending on which foot I step into the circle with, my teammates know who

I'm going to throw the ball to. It hardly ever gets intercepted. It's like a secret code between us that our opponents can't figure out.

My favourite is when I put my left foot in first. This means Lissa, who's playing Wing Attack today, does a dummy run in to pretend to get the ball and then quickly veers to the side. Tori, who's Wing Defence, darts into the spot where Lissa was to take it and passes it straight to Dani who lobs it into the net. I can't believe it, they fall for it every time! You'd think they'd wise up but they don't!

At the end of the game we've beaten them hollow, 14–2, and Mrs Waters is overjoyed. I do three cheers for the other side and three cheers for the umpire, shake hands with everyone and get ready to run. It's already gone four thirty.

'Well played, Captain!' says Mrs Waters, clapping me on the back. 'We'll have a quick debriefing in the changing room when the other team has left.'

'I've got to go, Miss!' I say desperately.

'It won't take long.'

But when I look inside the changing room it's heaving with excited, chattering girls from both schools who want to bond now the game is over.

I glance at the time again. If I leave now and they're running late as usual at the surgery, there's still a chance I can catch them before Mum's appointment. Then she can go in and have a proper chat with the doctor without having to worry about what the boys are up to. If I'm not there she might decide to cancel and go home instead.

I don't attempt to get changed, I just stuff my clothes into my bag and leg it as fast as I can.

By the time I get there it's five o'clock. The waiting room is crowded, it always is, but there's no sign of Mum and the boys. I stand in line to speak to the receptionist, kept waiting by a woman complaining about the time *she's* been kept waiting. Funny that.

'Comfort Campbell?' I ask when it's my turn at last. 'She had an appointment at four thirty. Has she left?'

The receptionist, looking thoroughly fed-up, consults her list. 'She's with the doctor now.'

'Can I go in?' I ask and she frowns at me. 'I want to get my brothers so my mum can talk to the doctor in private,' I explain and she nods at me curtly.

'That one over there. Next please!'

I walk over to the door she indicates, knock tentatively and push it open.

'Shall I take the boys . . .?' I say hesitantly, but a voice booms, 'What's this, not another one? Come in, come in, join the party!' The room is small and untidy with overflowing shelves, not a lot of floor space and a huge desk with a computer and lots of paper scattered all over it.

The voice, half-jolly, half-scary, belongs to a very large man with glasses on the end of his nose, who is sitting at the desk. I've never seen this doctor before. He looks hot and bothered like it's been a long day and his shirt has got wet patches under the arms. Yuck.

Mum is sat opposite him with Keneil on her lap and Marlon by her side, but the doctor is looking at the computer, not her.

'Headaches . . . tiredness . . .' he says, tapping away.

Behind him Devon says, 'What are those?' and points to a stack of phials with fluid inside them.

'Don't touch, young man,' warns the doctor. 'They're samples, ready to be collected for testing.'

Keneil leans forward and tugs gently at the stethoscope hanging round the doctor's neck.

'Ouch, steady on, young man!' says the doctor, sounding less jolly by the minute.

Keneil, thinking it's a game, tugs harder and, this time, succeeds in yanking the stethoscope off. The doctor roars in surprise and, immediately, Keneil's face falls and he starts bawling. Meanwhile, Devon, who can never resist touching anything, pulls out a particularly interesting specimen from the bottom of the sample pile and the whole stack of them goes crashing to the floor, making us all jump a mile.

The doctor lumbers to his feet and flings opens the door and I'm guessing he's going to chuck us all out but instead he bellows, 'NURSE!' Then he sits back down, rubs his hands over his sweaty face and turns his attention to Mum. 'So, you were saying . . . headaches . . . tiredness . . . Anything else?'

'I'm feeling a bit down to tell you the truth. I find myself getting angry easily . . .'

The doctor snorts and looks balefully at Devon and Keneil. 'I wonder why? Single mother, you say?'

Mum looks alarmed. 'Yes.'

'Got a job?'

'Three.'

He shakes his head and turns back to the computer. 'What do you expect? You must be worn out, woman.'

A nurse comes into the room, neat as a pin in her navy-blue uniform. Her eyes widen when she sees all the phials on the floor, but she bends down to pick them up without a word. I drop down to help her and so does Devon.

'I'm sorry,' he whispers and she smiles at him.

'Don't worry,' she says. 'These things happen.' She's nice. When she smiles she reminds me of someone.

'But that doesn't explain my clumsiness,' says Mum bravely. 'My fingers tingle all the time and I drop things . . .'

'Runs in the family!' barks the doctor, glaring at Devon, and he continues tapping away.

'She walked into a door and got a black eye!' I say, because I don't think he's taking her seriously enough. Mum frowns at me but at least he stops typing and peers at her over the top of his glasses.

'Is there a boyfriend around?'

What a weird question to ask.

'NO!' says Mum most indignantly, and suddenly I get where he's coming from. I feel sick. He thinks someone's hit her. Domestic abuse, that's what they call it. I've read about it in the paper.

'When would I have time for a boyfriend?' she snaps and he looks as if he believes her. Mum takes a deep breath and continues. 'My vision is blurred, you see,' she explains, but he's turned back to the screen. I don't think he's very computer literate.

The nurse gets to her feet and looks at Mum with concern. She's got kind eyes.

'Exhaustion,' he says, finding the save button and tapping it triumphantly. 'Three jobs, four kids. Hardly surprising.' He sounds like he's telling her off. 'You need a break. Is there someone who can take this lot off your hands for a while?'

This lot. It's obvious what he thinks of us. 'No,' says Mum flatly and starts gathering her things together. The doctor presses a few more buttons and the printer starts whirring. He tears off a prescription, scribbles on the bottom of it and hands it with a flourish to Mum.

'What's this for?' she asks.

'Sleeping tablets,' he says. 'Should do the trick.'

'But I don't need sleeping tablets,' she says. 'I told you. I'm tired all the time. It's hard to stay awake.'

'No wonder.' He makes it sound like it's all her fault. 'Take a week off work,' he adds. 'Put your feet up.'

'Chance would be a fine thing,' says Mum bitterly as she ushers us all out of the door. But he's stopped listening and is back on the computer.

Chapter 23

'That was a flaming waste of time!' grumbles Mum as we walk home together through the now dark streets. 'Sleeping tablets!' She crumples up the prescription and stuffs it into her pocket.

'I'm sorry I was late,' I say.

'Where were you anyway?' she says crossly and I stare at her in surprise.

'Netball match, remember? I told you!'

Her face looks stricken. 'Oh, Tash, I don't know what's the matter with me! My memory's terrible! How did it go?'

'We won,' I say curtly.

How could she forget? She *knew* how important it was to me. Lissa's mum put her daughter's netball match in pride of place on her calendar and came and watched her. Not mine. OK, Dani's mum wasn't there either but she was working, Dani said. Most of the time my mum was working and I didn't mind that. But today she hadn't even remembered it was on, even though we'd had a discussion about it last night.

That's how important I am to her.

'I'm sorry, darling,' she says, reading my mind. 'Well done, I'm proud of you.'

I don't even deign to reply.

We have tea when we get home and then Mum puts Keneil to bed and rushes off to work. I listen to the boys read then leave them in front of the telly while I settle down on my bed to do my English homework. Don't want any more detentions! After a while I hear noises coming from the kitchen. They can't be hungry again! Crossly I poke my head round the door. There's stuff everywhere. Two floury faces beam at me.

'What are you two up to?'

'Making a birthday cake for Mum.'

'D'you know what you're doing?'

'Sort of.'

I peer into the mixing bowl. It's full to the brim with a grey lumpy mixture.

'What did you put in it?'

'Sugar and flour and eggs and butter.'

'We've seen Mum do it loads of times.'

'And currants.'

'Yeah . . . and that spicy stuff.'

'What spicy stuff?'

'What Mum put in the Christmas cake.'

'Right.' I stare glumly into the bowl. 'Did you measure out the ingredients?'

They raise their eyes to me silently. I sigh heavily.

We throw away the stuff in the bowl because it looks disgusting and start again. Fortunately, there's just enough flour, sugar, butter and eggs left to make a Victoria sponge cake. Before long it's out of the oven and cooling. It smells delicious. I sandwich it together with the gooseberry jam from the market while the boys scrape the bowl.

'What can we decorate it with?' I ask.

'I know!' Devon dashes to his room and comes back with a bar of chocolate and a tube of Smarties in each hand.

'Where did you get those from?' I ask in surprise.

'He's got a secret stash,' says Marlon and Devon says, 'No, I haven't!'

I wonder where he's getting them from and immediately my mind flies to the sweetshop and the security guard. But I can't deal with this now so I say firmly, 'Stop arguing! Mum will be home soon!'

We melt the chocolate over a basin of hot water and spoon it over the top, smoothing it down with a knife. Soon it has cooled into thick chocolate icing. Then very, very carefully we pick out the word 'MUM' in Smarties, doing a letter each.

'It looks brilliant,' says Devon, smiling from ear to ear. 'Can we stay up and show Mum when she comes in?' He's a sweet boy really.

'No way!' I say. 'We're going to hide it till tomorrow,' and I stand on a chair and place it on the highest shelf of the kitchen cupboard out of harm's way.

Then Marlon says, 'Can we make cards for her?' and so we do, even though I've already bought one. And just as we finish we hear Mum's key in the door and both of them scamper off to bed clutching their cards while I sweep all the bits into the bin.

Mum's face is white with exhaustion. 'Put the kettle on, Tash, there's a good girl,' she says with a deep sigh and collapses on to the sofa. 'I'll just put my feet up for ten minutes and then we'll decide what we're having for tea tomorrow . . . Remind me, is Ali vegetarian?'

At least she remembered she was coming to tea! 'No. The others aren't either.' I give her a hug for being thoughtful and make her a nice cup of tea, taking a sneaky peek at the birthday cake while I'm waiting for the kettle to boil. I can't wait to see her face when she sees it!

When I take the tea in to her she's flat out. Poor Mum, she works so hard to make ends meet, no wonder she forgets things sometimes. I feel rotten for being cross with her earlier. I must be more understanding.

I fetch the duvet off her bed and tuck it round her. It's a shame to wake her. She's got tomorrow off so there'll be plenty of time to get things ready.

I drink the tea myself, turn the lights off and go to bed. I can't wait for tomorrow.

It's Mum's birthday and my friends are coming to tea!

Chapter 24

I'd meant to get up early in the morning before Mum woke me, what with it being her birthday. Plus, I'd still got some homework to finish off. But instead I sleep in.

When I wake up the sun is streaming through the window. I check the time on my watch and leap out of bed in shock.

Mum is still dead to the world on the sofa under the duvet. When I shake her she comes to, all bleary-eyed.

'Where am I?' she mumbles and her speech is slurred. She sounds like one of those people who sit around on benches all day drinking out of bottles. No wonder the Barbies thought she was an alkie!

'Mum! Wake up! We're late for school!'

She groans and sits upright, rubbing her eyes.

But, as she gets to her feet, she stumbles and has to grab on to me to stand up straight.

'Mum! Let go! I'll get into trouble if I'm late!'

She sits back down heavily and runs her hands through her hair. 'You go, pet,' she says. 'I'll see to the boys.'

I take her at her word and jump into my uniform and brush my teeth. 'Have something to eat!' she says but I just knock back a glass of milk because there's no time. I grab my bag and am rushing out the door before I remember.

'Happy birthday!' I say and she smiles at me. 'Oh, your card . . . it's . . .'

'Just go!' she says, flapping her hands at me. 'It can wait till tonight.'

'OK. See you later!'

I don't wait for the lift but tear downstairs and out through the front door as fast as I can, racing through the estate to the main road. Ahead of me I can see people getting on the bus. It's a much later one than I normally catch and twice as busy, packed full of kids going to the comp.

'Wait for me!' I yell. The last few boys at the back of the queue laugh at me and I curse. But then one of them hangs back, one foot on, one foot off the platform, and I realize he's keeping the bus waiting for me. I fling myself past him, press my pass on the machine, and collapse breathless into an empty seat. My saviour sits down beside me amid a storm of catcalls and piercing whistles from everyone else on the bus.

'Thanks!' I gasp, turning to face my knight in shining armour.

It's Ajay!

'My pleasure,' he says and grins. Lissa was right. Ajay is gorgeous. And he's completely different from what I first thought. Unlike most kids round here, he doesn't judge me as posh or stuck up just because I go to a different school. He doesn't take a blind bit of notice of his mates mocking us and before long they lose interest.

We chat about all sorts of stuff.

He says Marlon's a really good footballer for his age and I tell him how Devon loves to watch him break-dance and he's well pleased. I explain that Devon's not allowed out on the estate without Mum or me, but you know what kids are like and he agrees. He asks if I want him to keep an eye out for Devon and I agree. Then he tells me he's seen Devon with Mason Riley and he's trouble, and in the end I find myself explaining to him that I'm worried Devon's been nicking. He looks surprised.

'Nicking what?'

'Chocolate. I found out he's got a secret stash.'

'Aahh!' he says, looking a bit embarrassed. 'That's my fault. My mum works in the chocolate factory, you see. I get loads for free. I gave him some to stay away from Mason Riley!'

That was so nice of him! We talk about loads more stuff on our estate and agree about loads more things. He is soooo easy to talk to. And then, in what seems like seconds, we're at his school stop and everyone piles out except me. When the bus drives past him he looks up and waves at me. I wave at him back.

Then I can't stop smiling, all the way to school.

Chapter 25

Despite Ajay's help, I end up being seriously late for school. I miss registration altogether and have to sign in at the office. Then I go straight to my first lesson and, lucky for me, it's PE. I breathe a sigh of relief. After last night's win, I am definitely in Mrs Waters' good books. If it was science I'd be really for it from Miss Riddle. This reminds me that next lesson is English and I haven't finished my homework from last night. Well, I'll have to cross that bridge when I come to it. My English teacher, Miss Webb, who's also my form teacher, is really nice so I should be able to blag my way out of trouble.

Only it doesn't work out like that. None of it. Mrs Waters collars me and it's immediately obvious I am no longer flavour of the month.

'Why are you late, Tasheika Campbell?' she asks

as soon as I run on to the netball court and I know straight away I'm in trouble because teachers only ever use your full name and put their hands on their hips when they're cross with you. But before I can open my mouth she adds, 'And where did you get to last night? I thought I asked you to stay behind for a debriefing with everyone else?'

'Sorry, Miss –' I begin, but she cuts me dead.

'You're captain, remember?'

'Yes, Miss.'

'You should be setting an example to the others.'

'Yes, Miss.'

'You have some questions to answer, my girl,' she says, which I've kind of worked out. 'Report to me at lunchtime.'

'Yes, Miss,' I say miserably. And then I play rubbish because she's mad at me.

At breaktime I try desperately to do my homework but everyone keeps asking me why I was late and I just wish they'd shut up because I can't concentrate. I don't mean Ali and the others, I mean people like the Barbies whose noses are twitching like hounds after a fox. Then the bell goes and it's double English and things take a turn for the worse.

145

'Where were you this morning, Tasheika?' Miss Webb asks me as soon as I enter the room. But when I try to explain (what is it with teachers?) she says, 'Not now. Stay behind at the end of the lesson.'

Across the aisle I hear Georgia mutter, 'She is *so* dead!' And I know she's right because two teachers want to see me at lunchtime now and Miss Webb has still to find out I haven't done my homework.

When the bell goes for lunch I remain in my seat until everyone has gone. Then Miss Webb, who has been flicking through the pile of homework books on her desk says, 'What's going on, Tasheika?'

'Miss?'

My heart sinks as she ticks off my misdemeanours on her fingers.

'One. You missed registration this morning.

'Two. I hear you disobeyed Mrs Waters last night and left school without permission.

'Three. I gather you failed to do homework for Miss Riddle.

'Four. I've checked your English homework and it's incomplete.

'Five. Mrs Waters tells me that though you can

be quite brilliant at netball you are not always consistent and you do not take the responsibilities of captain seriously enough.'

'Yes I do!' I say, stung to the core, but she ignores me.

'Six. I have noticed as your form teacher that you frequently make it to school by the skin of your teeth and dash off as soon as the bell goes.'

'Yeah, but that's not breaking any rules, is it?' It's a genuine question but it comes out sounding rude even though I don't mean it to. My mum would go mad if she heard me talking to a teacher like this.

Miss Webb doesn't get cross though. Instead, she regards me gravely. Then she says in a gentle voice, 'What's wrong, Tash? Is there anything you would like to talk to me about?'

That's nearly my undoing. Tell me off and I can keep a grip. Be nice to me and I fall apart. There's a lump in my throat and tears are pricking my eyelids and threatening to splash down my cheeks.

I want to talk to you, nice, kind Miss Webb. I want to tell you, Yes, actually, there is something wrong and please, Miss, can you make it better?

But I can't because I'm not allowed to. It's a

secret. Mum says we mustn't tell anyone. So I sit there mutely glaring at her because that's the only way I can stop myself crying.

'Go and get your lunch,' she says in the end. 'I'll deal with you later.'

I scrape my chair back and flounce out of the classroom because if I don't keep this stroppiness up, I'll dissolve. I'm starving hungry, I've had nothing but a glass of milk this morning, but I don't go to lunch, there's no point. I haven't brought anything to eat.

And, anyway, Mrs Waters wants to see me in her office.

Chapter 26

'You're late!' she snaps. 'Again!'

Mrs Waters is mad. Boiling mad. Like steam-coming-out-of-her-ears mad.

'Sorry, Miss,' I say, but she's not listening.

'How dare you run off last night when I specifically told you to remain behind! Who do you think you are?'

I open my mouth but I think this must be one of those rhetorical questions teachers ask because she lobs another one at me before I can answer. 'Do you take *anything* seriously?'

'Yes, Miss!'

'You could have fooled me! You do what you feel like as far as I can see –'

'No I don't!' I say, because it's so not true.

Her eyes flash and she lets loose a barrage of accusations, each one wounding me as it hits its target. 'You may be a good player, Tasheika, but you've got a lot to learn! You're inconsistent; I never know what to expect from you. You blow hot and cold from one day to the next. There's more to being a captain, you know, than mere talent –'

'I *know* that!'

'You can't be trusted –'

'Yes I can!'

'You're unreliable –'

'No I'm not!'

'I thought you loved netball –'

'I *do* love netball!

'I thought I could count on you –'

'You *can* count on me!'

'I don't think so! You're one of the least dependable girls I've ever met!'

I gasp at the sheer injustice of it all and we glare at each other. We're two dogs circling each other, alert and wary. She, top dog, ready for the next nip. Me, underdog, hackles rising.

Suddenly she barks, 'You've got one minute to come up with one good reason why I should allow you to remain as captain.'

I bite my lip. What can I say?

I want to explain to her. I want her to know I

am dependable. I want to tell her just how much responsibility I have at home. But I can't. I stand there silent, my eyes to the floor, listening to the seconds on the clock counting down.

'Look at me, Tash. One reason,' she says and her voice is softer now, almost pleading.

I can't look at her. Not if she's being nice to me. I can't speak because if I do the truth will come out.

I don't have a voice any more. Mum's taken it from me.

I raise my eyes, but instead of looking at her I gaze out through the window to the netball court in the distance, fighting my tears. Then, slowly and deliberately, I shrug my shoulders.

'I don't like your attitude, young lady,' her voice rattles out, hard as stone again.

And then she strips me of the captaincy.

Chapter 27

I'd been so looking forward to my friends coming home to tea and meeting my family at last. But, after the day I've had, I don't want them to any more. Everything in my life is going wrong so why should tonight be different?

I haven't told them yet I'm not captain any more. I can't. I'm too ashamed.

Lissa's so excited she's doing my head in. You'd think she'd never been invited anywhere for tea before. Suddenly I feel cold. Lissa will be chosen as netball captain now, she's bound to be.

It's not fair. Lissa gets everything she wants.

Everything *I* want.

When the bus arrives, she leads her way to the back and starts to strip off her school uniform. We stare at her in amazement. 'What are you doing?'

'Ta-dahhh!' She delves into her bag and pulls out a new outfit, holding it up triumphantly for us to inspect. I breathe in sharply. It's gorgeous.

'Oh I get it,' says Dani. 'She's hoping she'll bump into Ajay. She's dressing to impress.'

She certainly is. She denies it so loudly it's obvious.

Dani grins. 'Might as well get changed too then,' she says, and the next thing they're all wriggling out of their uniforms and into their fave outfits: Lissa's, designer-minted; Ali's, ethical-skinted; Dani's, boy jeans and checked shirt. And then they get really silly and giggly, even Dani, and all the way home they're chat, chat, chat to each other non-stop and I just wish they'd shut up.

I lean my forehead against the cold window-pane, feeling alone and bleak.

'You all right, Tash?' asks Ali, nudging me in the ribs. I ignore her and she gives me a funny look then carries on messing about with the others. They start up a daft game of waving to passers-by out of the back window to see who they can get to wave back. You'd swear they'd never been on a bus before.

I don't feel like joining in. Here I am, taking

my three closest friends home for tea for the first time, and I'm dreading it. I think back to the day the letter came to say I'd passed for Riverside Academy. I remember Mum opening it and whooping for joy. 'You've done it, you clever girl!' she'd said, waving it in the air. 'This is your passport out of here!'

I'd wondered what she meant. Like, I was off to a better world? I'd never really thought about where I lived until then. OK, the estate was noisy and there was lots of litter and the lifts never worked and Mum didn't like Devon playing out because he was easily led and some people you knew you had to avoid. But it was home and it was all I knew.

But now I know it's different from what my new friends are used to. For a start, unlike them, I live in a flat, not a house. Ali lives on an estate too, but in a semi-detached house with a garden, and Dani lives in a terraced house in a street. Lissa lives in a really posh house in a really posh road and Ali says it's like something out of a magazine, with a piano and shelves full of books, and she knows because she's been there.

So? We've got books even if we haven't got a piano (you would never get it up the stairs even if we could afford it). I love our flat – it's light and bright up there in the sky away from the world below and Mum keeps it really nice.

Most of the time. Except lately when things have been getting on top of her and she's not been well. This morning I'd left her half-asleep on the sofa in the clothes she'd slept in all night with the boys still in bed.

Now I feel nervous. What if she's let them stay off school because we all overslept? What if she's forgotten all about the party and my friends coming to tea? Her memory's rubbish lately. What if she'd just gone back to sleep and left the boys to it? The place would be wrecked! Eek!

I don't want to do this any more. If only I could cancel the party.

Chapter 28

We get off the bus and walk through the estate, me silently praying that Devon hasn't escaped from the flat and is on the rampage with Mason Riley. There's no sign of him but a group of older kids is hanging about outside our block and they turn to stare at us. I look away. I feel awkward and conspicuous with my new friends and even though I'm still in my school uniform, I'm glad they've changed out of theirs.

But then a voice says, 'Hi, Tasheika! Hey, it's Lissa, yeah? Remember me?' and Ajay detaches himself from the group to high-five us both. I am so glad to see him. I'm not the only one. Beside me, Lissa beams from ear to ear.

I introduce Ali and Dani to Ajay and he responds by introducing the rest of the gang to my friends. The sour girls aren't there today, thank goodness; it's mainly people who were a few years older than me at primary school, only they look different now because they've grown up. Everyone smiles and says 'Hi!' to each other.

'Do you know my friend, Austen Penberthy?' Ali asks Ajay. 'He goes to your school. He's in Year Seven.'

He turns to the others. 'Isn't that the nerdy kid with the glasses who's always bleating on about saving the planet?'

'Don't be rude, Ajay!' squeals a girl and he adds quickly, 'No offence!'

'That's him,' says Ali, not in the least bit offended. She's used to Austen being mocked for his forthright opinions. Even her dad calls him Earthy Penberthy. Ali was mocked too, by the Barbies, when she started at Riverside because she shares the same ethical views as Austen. Until she put on the brilliant 'Fashion with a Conscience' show practically single-handed, that is, which improved her street cred no end. Then, when they found out her sister was Alana de Silva, she became the hottest girl in the school.

'I think he's cute!' says the girl.

'He's a freaking brain-box,' says a boy and Ali smiles with pleasure.

We chat a bit more then say goodbye. In the lobby Lissa says, 'Oh it's so friendly round here; you're so lucky! There's no one young where I live,' and I forgive her for fancying Ajay. She presses the button for the lift and, lo and behold, it's working for once and, what's even better, it's not in the least bit smelly, it's been freshly cleaned. And when the doors open at the tenth floor, Marlon and Devon and Keneil jump out and shout 'SURPRISE!' They've been lying in wait for us with balloons and streamers, and everyone screams with delight. But, best of all, the door to our flat is wide open and Mum is standing there looking cool and gorgeous. She's dressed up too in skinny jeans and a new vest top, and she's wearing big dangly earrings and a great big smile as she welcomes us all in.

'Wow!' says Lissa, staring at her with undisguised admiration. 'Is that your mum? She's so young!'

'Wow!' says Dani, running over to the window. 'Look at the view from up here! It's amazing!'

'Wow!' says Ali, gazing at the brightly painted yoghurt pots and bells made from egg cartons hung round the walls and the shiny stars made out of foil stuck on the window. 'Who made all these amazing decorations?'

'We did,' says Devon proudly. 'For Christmas. But we've recycled them for Mum's party.'

'Wicked!' says Ali, who is totally into recycling. I slip away to change into *my* fave jeans and top and when I come back everyone's standing around sipping tall drinks through straws, and they've got pieces of fruit and tiny umbrellas and ice in them, like proper cocktails.

'Your mum is so cool,' whispers Lissa. 'She looks like your older sister!' and suddenly I feel really, really proud, especially when she adds moodily, 'My mum's ancient!'

After that we eat pizza and there are not one, not two, not three, not four, but FIVE kinds to choose from! Ham and Pineapple, Americano, Four Cheese, Margherita and Red Hot Chilli, plus garlic bread and posh crisps and coleslaw and bowls full of fresh green salad. I think Mum must have raided the CHRISTMAS as well as the BIRTHDAYS tin for all this.

'These are really good!' mumbles Ali, her mouth full, and we all burst out laughing.

'What?' she says blankly, and it's little Keneil who takes pity on her and points out the long string of mozzarella dangling from her lips to the rest of the pizza on her plate, because the rest of us are giggling too much. There's so much pizza we can't finish it all even though Lissa eats twice as much as the rest of us. I don't know where she puts it. But in the end even she's groaning.

After that we sit down and play Pass the Parcel.

'I thought you were joking!' I say to Mum, a bit embarrassed at first, but the others are totally up for it. We have a laugh because both Lissa and Devon are really competitive; I'm not kidding, they're as bad as each other, hanging on to the parcel in case the music stops instead of passing it on. In the end, Dani wins, and it's this really girly hairslide with a pink fabric flower on top. You should see her face, it's hilarious!

'Give it to someone else,' suggests Mum.

'Me!' says Devon, which makes us all collapse laughing again, especially when he puts it in his hair and prances cheekily around the room pretending to be a girl! Then Dani and Marlon go outside to kick a football to shouts of 'Party Poopers!' while the rest of us play more games for prizes.

After a while Devon gets bored and peers over the balcony. 'Look!' he says. 'They're playing footie with Ajay and his mates. Mum, can I go and play too?'

We race to the balcony and call down to them. They wave back and Ajay cups his hands and yells up, 'Come and join us!'

Of course Lissa immediately wants to then as well as Devon.

'OK,' says Mum. 'Just this once. Look after Keneil, Tash.' But I don't need to. Keneil's already grabbed hold of Ali's hand – she's his new best friend since she gave him the sweets she won as a prize in Dead Lions. We have a fab game of footie on the forecourt below our flat, all of us together: Ajay and his mates, me and my mates and my brothers, even little Keneil who plays in goal with Ali. And Dani's right, you know, football *is* fun, even if we do bend the rules a bit.

In the end, Mum leans over the balcony and calls us in because it's getting so dark. So we have a race back up to the flat: Ali and Keneil in the lift, me, Dani, Lissa, Marlon and Devon up the stairs. And the stairs win!

'This is the best birthday party ever!' says Lissa, gasping for breath, her face hot and sweaty. 'I don't want to go home.' And even though it's obvious she fancies Ajay, and he's *my* friend, not hers, I could kiss her.

I am *sooooooooooo* happy!

Suddenly I remember that I haven't told her yet, nor Mum, nor anyone, that I've been stripped of the captaincy and, maybe because I'm already winded from the race upstairs, the pain of it takes my breath away.

But after a while I get used to it again.

Nothing's ever going to be perfect, is it?

Chapter 29

The day should have ended there, right then. Or maybe it could have gone on a little bit longer, until I lit the candles on our surprise cake and my brothers carried it in for Mum, just as Ali's dad and Lissa's mum turned up. We all sang 'Happy Birthday' to Mum and she looked so happy. It was magic. She blew out the candles and made a wish and then we had to light them again so first Keneil and then Devon could blow them out too, even though Devon pretended he was far too old for all that.

Everyone has a slice, even Ali's dad and Lissa's mum. Ali's dad accepts a big piece straight away, but Lissa's mum says, 'No thank you,' sounding like Devon, like she's way too old for Victoria sponge with chocolate and Smartie icing but she wants to really.

'Oh go on,' says Mum, refusing to take no for an answer, just like she did with Devon. She thrusts the plate into her hand. 'The kids made it for me.'

'Really?' says Mrs Hamilton, and I feel a pang for her because I get the impression no one's ever made her a surprise birthday cake. She takes a polite nibble, then says, 'It's delicious,' and scoffs the lot.

'They made me these cards as well,' says Mum, plucking them off the mantelpiece.

'What thoughtful children you have,' says Mrs Hamilton, studying them carefully, and Mum smiles at her, proud and pleased.

I think Lissa's mum is much nicer than she looks, even if she does sound like the queen. They leave soon after. Lissa thanks Mum politely but while they're waiting for the lift we can hear her complaining loudly to her mum that she's the first one to go and it's not fair.

Ali leaves next. 'I've had the best time ever!' she says, flinging her arms round my neck. Keneil, in turn, flings his arms round her knees, refusing to let her go.

Mum laughs. 'You must come again! I think you've made a friend!'

Ali's eyes shine. 'Yes please!'

Ali and her dad leave with lots of hugs and goodbyes and invitations on both sides and then there's only Dani and us left.

'You go and watch telly and I'll clear up,' says Mum.

'Mum! It's your birthday!'

'We'll help!' offers Dani.

'Go on with you!' says Mum. 'I'll be fine!'

And she looked fine, she really did. Bit tired, but that was to be expected. I was so proud of her at that moment. Proud to have such a pretty, lively, capable, fun mum who was only just thirty-three and looked young enough to be my sister, young enough to be Lissa's mum's daughter.

Dani and I do as we're told and snuggle up together on the sofa under my duvet with Keneil between us doing his hot-water-bottle thing while Mum starts stacking plates from the table and carrying them into the kitchen. A few minutes later the bell goes and Devon jumps up to open the door.

'Ohhhh!' complains Dani. 'That'll be my mum! I want to stay a bit longer.'

I wriggle my toes with pleasure. My friends

have had such a good time at my place, not one of them wants to go home. There was nothing to worry about after all.

This is the best day ever.

'Come in,' says Devon politely. I turn to say hello to Dani's mum. Our eyes meet and mine open wide in surprise. I recognize this woman.

But, before I can say anything, there's a clashing, smashing, crashing noise from the kitchen, followed by a dull thud and I leap off the sofa to see what's going on.

Mum's on the kitchen floor face down, surrounded by smashed plates and bits of food. She's out cold. Keneil takes one look at her and starts howling. Behind me I hear Marlon moan, Dani gasp and Devon shout, '*Mum!*' I drop to my knees beside her and touch her arm, but she doesn't respond, and I can feel the panic rising in me. I don't know what to do.

'Let me through,' says a firm, calm voice. 'I'm a nurse.'

Dani's mum bends down beside me for the second time in two days.

Dani's mum is the nurse from the practice

yesterday, the one with the kind eyes. I knew her as soon as I saw her.

I have never been so pleased to see anyone in my whole life.

Chapter 30

Mum's home from hospital. They've not finished with her though. She's been having loads of tests to see what's wrong with her.

They want to find out why she's tired all the time, or suffering from 'fatigue', as they call it.

Why her balance is bad and she keeps dropping things and walking into walls and falling over.

Why her vision blurs and her words slur.

Why she forgets things and finds it hard to concentrate.

Why her leg keeps going to sleep and her fingers tingle and she gets pins and needles.

Why she's in pain.

'I thought it was me overdoing things,' she explains to Pam who is sitting on the sofa next to her. Pam is Dani's mum and Mum's new best friend. She's really kind. She took us home with her after Mum went off in the ambulance. Mum had come round by then and was flatly refusing to go to hospital until Pam said we could stay with her.

We slept at Dani's house for the next five nights. Dani's sister Jade went in with her and I slept in a Z bed alongside them. The boys slept in Jade's room – only during the night Keneil usually found his way into my bed! I didn't mind and neither did Dani's mum. He was missing Mum. We all were.

But it's OK, she's home again now.

'Well, maybe that's all it is,' says Pam comfortingly. 'But at least you're being properly investigated, so if there is anything wrong they should find it.'

'What then?' says Mum, looking worried.

Pam pats her knee. 'We'll cross that bridge when we come to it.'

Pam makes me feel safe. '*We*,' she said, like she'll be around to help us. She's already helped us loads: looking after us, ringing all Mum's jobs to explain she won't be in for a while, sorting out benefit payments to tide us over while Mum's off work. And tomorrow she's going with Mum to get the results of her tests.

I hope Mum's passed.

Chapter 31

Mum passed her tests but not in the way I expected. They've found out what she's got.

It's MS. My mum's got MS. Multiple Sclerosis. It's a disease of the central nervous system. It means 'many scars' but they're invisible ones, deep inside. Anyone can get it at any time but it's most common between the ages of twenty and forty.

Mum explained it all to us when she got home, with Pam chipping in to make it clearer. Mum's eyes were red as if she'd been crying but she was strangely calm and peaceful, like all the tension and worry had drained away with the tears.

'What it means is messages have trouble getting ⌐gh from my brain.'

'' the time,' says Pam quietly.

Marlon.

passes messages through your

spinal cord to the rest of your body to make it work.'

'What's your spinal cord?' asks Devon.

'This.' Mum whips up Keneil's shirt and runs her hand down his backbone.

'It tickles!' says my little brother, wriggling like mad, so Mum tickles him even more.

'But in your mum's case the messages aren't always getting through,' adds Pam.

'Why not?' persists Marlon who likes to understand everything.

'Because sometimes my spinal cord doesn't work properly,' says Mum.

'It's a bit like talking on a mobile phone when you're on the train,' explains Pam. 'One minute you're chatting away happily to someone and the next minute the train's entered a tunnel and your phone cuts out. That's what's happening to your mum.'

'So your phone's not working properly?' asks Devon.

'In a way, yes,' says Mum.

'And that's why your leg wouldn't work?' asks Marlon.

'Yes.'

'And why you dropped things?' I add.

'Yes.'

Now I feel really bad, remembering how I'd yelled at her, called her a clumsy idiot, told her to go away.

'And why you sounded funny sometimes?' says Devon.

Mum nods sadly.

'Is that why you . . .?' says Keneil who thinks it's a game but he can't think of anything else so he covers his mouth with both hands and giggles and it makes us all smile.

'Can you get a new one?' asks Devon.

'What, a new leg?' says Mum, still smiling.

'Or a new brain?' says Marlon.

'Or a new spinal cord?' says me.

'No, a new phone,' says Devon. 'Then I can have your old one. I don't mind if it doesn't work properly.'

Mum looks at Pam and they both burst out laughing.

'See,' says Pam. 'I told you it would be fine.'

It might be fine for everyone else. But it's not fine for me.

That night I get out of bed and slip quietly into Mum's room.

'Mum?'

'Tash? Can't you sleep?'

'No.'

'Come on.' She lifts up the corner of her duvet and I crawl in beside her, turning automatically on to my side. She curls up behind me in our favourite position, so I'm sort of sitting on her knees with her arm round me like when I was little, only we're lying down in bed.

'Mum?'

'Yes?'

I don't know how to ask this question, so in the end I just blurt it out and hold my breath. 'Are you going to die?'

'Not of MS,' she says immediately, 'if that's what you're afraid of.' I let my breath out. 'I hope I'm going to live till I'm old.'

'How old?'

'Really old. As old as Mad Maggie! Older!' Both of us start giggling at the thought of my mum shuffling around the market in smelly clothes shouting rude words at everyone like Mad Maggie does and the tight knot of fear that has lodged in my throat ever since she told us she had MS starts to dissolve.

After a while I say, 'Is it going to get worse?'

She pauses for a moment, collecting her thoughts.

'Be honest!' I plead.

'OK. It's hard to predict. Sometimes it will. But sometimes it will get better too. They've got lots of things to help me.'

'Like what?'

'Drugs for the pain and the spasms. Physio, massage, yoga to help me stay supple and improve my balance.' She gives a little chuckle. 'Hey, Tash, I always wanted to go to yoga but I never had the time or money before. I can go now I'm not working.'

'But . . .' The fear of Mum dying has gone, but now there's a new one to replace it. 'What about money?'

'You can get yoga on the National Health if you need it!'

'I don't mean yoga! I mean, what will we do for money to live on if you don't go back to work?' I see before me a shelf with a row of tins marked WATER, ELECTRICITY, SCHOOL, FOOD, CLOTHES, BIRTHDAYS and CHRISTMAS — all of them empty.

She's silent for a while, thinking. Then she says, 'I will go back eventually, I'm sure. But not for a while. I need a rest.'

'But –' I turn round to face her in the darkness – 'how will we manage?' I feel terrible saying this but if Mum doesn't work we're going to starve. 'What's going to happen to us?'

'We'll be fine,' she says soothingly but I can feel panic rising inside me as problems loom over my head like thunder clouds.

'But, Mum, what if you have to go back into hospital? I'll have to look after everyone again and I can't do it. You told me I mustn't tell anyone but it's hard, Mum, it's really hard! I get into trouble at school if I don't get my homework done. I'm falling behind.'

'It's OK,' says Mum, stroking my arm, but I brush her off and sit bolt upright in bed. I'm in a state now and I can't stop. It all comes out in a rush.

'It's not OK! What about netball? I didn't want to tell you this, Mum, but you know I'm captain? You were dead proud of me when I was made netball captain, weren't you? Well, I'm not any more. Captain, I mean. Mrs Waters took it off me because I wasn't doing it properly. I couldn't, I had to rush off, you see, to get the boys when you were at the doctor's. I was always rushing off. She said I couldn't be relied on. Everyone thinks I'm flaky now, they think I don't care! But I do care, I care a lot.' Tears start spilling down my cheeks. 'I'm sorry, Mum, I know what you said, but I don't know if I can keep all this a secret any more!'

Mum sighs. 'Poor, Tash. You don't have to.' She reaches over and switches on her bedside light, bathing the room in a soft orange glow. 'Come here,' she says, taking me in her arms and I feel her cheek wet against mine. 'It's time you and I had a proper talk.'

Chapter 32

It's the evening after the second netball match. The other team were good and we had to have our wits about us. Lissa was captain. Today she played Centre and I was Goal Attack. We played the centre-pass and dummy-run trick again but they wised up to it after a while. We still beat them though. Just. I scored the winning goal just as the whistle blew for the end of the game. You couldn't hear it for the cheering!

I'm full to the brim with happiness. I'm so proud of the team and my amazing friends. (And me!) And the brilliant thing is Mrs Waters has decided to give each one of us a game as captain and when she's seen us all in the role she's going to choose afterwards. So I'm in with a chance again. I've just got to prove to her I *am* dependable!

Ali has stayed behind to watch and she's as excited as the rest of us. I wish she could be in the team too. Maybe one day.

Best of all, the icing on the cake, Mum was there to watch me. It's the first time she's ever seen me play. She came with Pam and it's the first time Pam has seen Dani play netball too.

'Made a nice change to see you passing a netball around instead of kicking a football, young lady,' she says at the end, giving her daughter a hug. Dani pulls a face but I think she's pleased really.

Ali's mum comes along after the match to give her a lift home. Lissa's mum is here, of course. She introduces Ali's mum to my mum and my mum introduces Pam to them and soon they're busy chatting away together nineteen to the dozen like old buddies.

Then Ali's mum says, 'Look, why don't we all go to McDonald's to celebrate the win?' which is really nice of her because Ali wasn't even playing.

And Lissa's mum says, 'What a good idea! My treat. No, I insist!' which totally surprises me because apparently she's into really healthy eating. Lissa looks as if all her birthdays and Christmases have rolled into one.

Ali looks uneasy. 'I'm not sure McDonald's is an ethically responsible company.'

'Oh, don't worry,' says Pam. 'I hear they're working hard to make a positive contribution to global concerns,' and Ali cheers up and agrees to come with us.

As we're walking down the road I hear Ali's mum whisper to Pam, 'Is that true?'

'I have no idea,' Pam whispers back. 'It worked though.' And Ali's mum laughs.

In the restaurant we sit at separate tables: girls on one, mums on another. Both tables are pretty noisy but I'd say the mums are louder, especially Mrs Hamilton. They're definitely not paying any attention to us, that's for sure. My mum's even on her phone, like a teenager!

'Your mum looks really well,' says Lissa indistinctly, taking a huge mouthful of cheeseburger.

'You'd never think she had MS,' says Dani who knows a bit about these things seeing as her mum's a nurse.

'Why didn't you tell us?' asks Ali, sounding a bit reproachful. What she really means is, *Why didn't you tell me?*

'I didn't know,' I say, tucking into my chips.

'But you knew something was wrong with her,' Lissa points out. 'All those symptoms. You must've been worried sick.'

'I was.'

'The Barbies said she was drunk,' recalls Dani scathingly. 'Shows how much they know. Like, how stupid are they?'

They're not the only ones I think to myself, remembering with shame how I searched the flat for evidence of my mum's secret drinking. I confessed to her what I'd done the night we had our talk and she'd laughed and said she didn't blame me and not to worry.

'We could've helped,' says Ali, and the others nod in agreement.

'I know,' I say, feeling really bad. 'But Mum made us promise we wouldn't tell anyone she was ill.'

'Why?' asks Dani. 'It's not like it's something to be ashamed of!'

'You said we weren't to keep anything from each other, remember? You were the one who called us the No Secrets Club,' Ali reminds me, and now I feel even more guilty.

'Yeah, maybe we should call ourselves the Secrets Club instead,' says Dani.

'Why?' asks Lissa, sharp as a knife. 'Have you got a secret?'

'No!' says Dani, quick as a flash. 'Have you?'

'No!'

'Shush, you two, I'm trying to explain. It's complicated.' I look across at the mums' table then sigh deeply and push my fries away. 'OK, it's like this. My mum was brought up in care, you see. She never had a proper family. When my dad left she had to bring us up all on her own. She worked really hard to look after us. When I passed for Riverside Academy, my mum was over the moon.'

'So was mine,' says Ali.

'And mine,' says Lissa and Dani in unison.

'She saw it as a passport to a better life than the one she'd had. She wants me to go to uni, get a good job. She wants me to become a politician or a doctor or a lawyer or something.'

'So does mine,' they all say.

Me: 'I may try to be prime minister one day for her sake. But personally I think I'd rather be someone like Alana de Silva. It's more fun.'

Ali: 'I want to be a conservationist.'

Dani: 'I want to be a professional footballer.'

Lissa: 'Actually, I wouldn't mind being a lawyer.'

Then Ali says, 'But I still don't get why you

kept it a secret from us that your mum was ill.'

'Well, when Mum got sick and started falling over and stuff she was really worried. She had no one else to turn to, you see. When they kept her in hospital the first time we had to pretend my dad was still at home.'

'Why?'

'I didn't really understand why. I just knew we must never, ever tell anyone we'd been left on our own. But now I know, she explained it all to me the other night: it was because she was afraid.'

Ali: 'Afraid?'

Dani: 'Afraid of what?'

Lissa: 'Or who?'

'The authorities. She thought we'd be split up and taken into care, like she was, if they found out there was no one to look after us. But she didn't tell us that at the time. She didn't want to frighten us. She just made us promise not to tell anyone or she'd get into trouble.'

'So who *did* look after you?'

'Me.'

Three pairs of eyes open wide.

'Respect!' says Dani.

'It wasn't too bad,' I say modestly. 'I'm used to looking after the boys.'

'Is that why you were always late?'

'I wasn't *always* late.'

'And why you never wanted to meet up at the weekend?' asks Ali.

'I *did* want to. But I was needed at home.'

She looks relieved. 'I thought it was me you didn't want to be with.'

'Don't be daft!'

Then Lissa says thoughtfully, 'So that explains why sometimes you were a bit rubbish at netball –'

Ali: 'Lissa!'

'I said "sometimes"! Most of the time she was awesome!' Then Lissa looks at me, stricken. 'I'm really, really sorry, Tash. I thought you just couldn't be bothered.'

'That's all right. You didn't know. Nobody did. Anyway, it's all sorted now. Dani's mum helped us. There's loads of help out there for people like us but Mum never knew. We've got a social worker to provide support for us to stay together as a family and a care worker helping out with the boys. She's giving them their tea this minute. I can stay at school as long as I like now. And people on the estate have been really good since they found out . . .'

My voice trails away as four boys walk through

the door. Four boys in descending order of height like steps on a staircase. They could all be brothers, they look so alike, but actually only three of them are. The other one is my friend.

'Hi,' grins Ajay as Keneil rushes over to our table and throws his arms round Ali. Marlon hangs back shyly as Dani high-fives Devon.

'Hi!' says Lissa and moves up to make room for Ajay, but he pulls up a seat next to me so Marlon slips in beside her instead.

I turn to Ajay. 'What are you doing here?'

His smile broadens. 'A little bird told us you were here and invited us to the party.' He nods over to the next table where Mum's smile is as wide as his. So that's who she was on her phone to!

Beside her, Lissa's mum regards him with interest. 'So that's Ajay,' she says. 'I've heard Melissa mention him.'

Lissa's face flushes.

'Tell me, Comfort,' continues Mrs Hamilton in her posh, plummy voice, 'is he Tasheika's young man?'

My face sizzles and my body goes rigid like I've been turned to stone.

'No, no,' I hear Mum saying. 'He's just a friend. I asked him to bring the boys along to join in the treat. I hope you don't mind. He's been so helpful . . .'

I'm afraid to move. But when I do Ajay is turned away from us, concentrating on the menu board. I don't think he heard Lissa's mum. The others did though. Dani and Ali have caught each other's eye and are sniggering, while Lissa is studying her empty ketchup pack, turning it round and round as if it's the most fascinating thing she's ever seen in her life.

'What's so funny?' asks Ajay, turning back.

'Nothing!' I say quickly, frowning at my friends.

He gets to his feet, stuffing his hand in his back pocket. 'Coke, bruvs?'

The boys jump down from the table and go to the counter with him to get their drinks.

Immediately, Dani leans over towards me. 'Tell me, Tasheika,' she says in a voice exactly like Mrs Hamilton's. 'Is Ajay really your *young man*?'

'No!'

'Yeah, right!' she scoffs, but in a nice way.

'Anyone can tell a mile off he's mad about you, Tash,' says Ali, smiling.

'It's true,' says Lissa with a resigned sigh, losing interest at last in the ketchup. 'Lucky thing!'

'Get lost!' I say. 'He's just a mate, that's all.

Like you lot!' But I can feel myself grinning from ear to ear.

Lissa groans theatrically. 'He's not a bit like us lot. He's gorgeous.'

'And we're ugly, is that what you mean?' says Dani. 'Whatever makes you say that?'

Then she pulls that face, the one where she crosses her eyes and sticks her tongue out of the side of her mouth, which is soooo funny. Ali copies her and then Lissa does, so I do too.

And then we notice Mrs Hamilton staring at us in surprise and we all fall about laughing.

Suddenly I feel as if a weight has been lifted from my shoulders. I was wrong. Sometimes, for a brief moment in time, things can be perfect. I'm me again. Happy, smiley Tash, without a care in the world.

'What's going on?' asks Ajay, coming back to the table with a tray full of Cokes, my brothers trailing after him.

'Nothing!' we all chorus.

He looks at us sceptically, eyebrows raised, then he grins. 'Girls!' he says cheerfully, shaking his head. 'Girls and their secrets!'

No More
Secrets

The Secrets Club

Alice's secret is out and now so is Tash's.
The friends have promised
NO MORE SECRETS!
But can they keep to it? Could Lissa
or Dani be hiding something too?

Don't miss the next book in the
Secrets Club series coming soon.

Are YOU in the Secrets Club? Join up at
www.secretsclubbooks.com